BEACHSIDE BEGINNINGS

MARIGOLD ISLAND BOOK TWO

FIONA BAKER

Copyright © 2021 by Fiona Baker

All rights reserved.

No part of this publication may be reproduced, distributed, or transmitted in any form, including photocopying, recording, or other electronic or mechanical methods, without the prior written permission of the publisher, except in the case of brief quotations for reviews or certain other noncommercial uses.

This is a work of fiction. Any resemblance to actual people, living or dead, or actual events is purely coincidental.

CHAPTER ONE

Angela Collins still couldn't get over how beautiful the water surrounding Marigold Island was, even though she and her younger sister Brooke took walks on the beach several times a week. The sea was a wide expanse of rich blue, glittering where the midmorning light hit it, occasionally interrupted by a boat drifting by.

Tucked between Nantucket and Martha's Vineyard, Marigold was a cozy and welcoming place all year round, but Angela was particularly fond of the summer months like these.

The late June air was still slightly cool even though the sun was shining down on her shoulders, and it felt clean in her lungs. She hadn't realized just how big of a difference there was between the air in

Philadelphia, where she had lived until a few months ago, and here.

It was one of many turns her life had taken recently. If someone had told her a year ago that she would give up her job as an interior decorator to purchase, renovate, and re-open an old inn on Marigold Island with her childhood best friend, Lydia Walker, all while debating whether to get a divorce, Angela would have laughed.

Her life before had been incredibly busy in Philadelphia, constantly juggling work and family without ever catching a breath. She had loved her job, but now that she had some distance from it, she realized that the pace hadn't been great for her in the long run.

Philadelphia's pace was like the salads she often used to grab from the place around the corner from her office—fast, good enough at the moment, but ultimately not all that satisfying. Marigold's pace was like savoring a delicious meal with family over the span of a few hours, something she had done frequently since her move to the island.

Now that she was living closer to family and was essentially her own boss, she had more balance. She was very busy, sure, but she could relax by walking along the beach like this or by having dinner with her family. Her parents could take Jake for an afternoon if she needed to spend more time at the inn or if she just wanted a break. She was able to spend more time with friends too.

"Breakfast service went well today, I think," Brooke said, drawing Angela from her thoughts. "Almost as well as the grand opening party did."

"Yeah. I think we're finally getting the hang of it." Angela let out a sigh of relief.

The inn had held its grand opening celebration a few days ago, which had gone incredibly well. It felt like nearly half the town had shown up to support them, nibbling on incredible fresh food and listening to one of the few local bands the island had. The lead-up to the party and the opening celebration had been stressful, and the pressure had only let up a small amount in the days after.

The learning curve of running the inn day-to-day was very steep, but they were keeping up.

Well, mostly.

Angela sometimes thought she had everything done, only to wake up in the middle of the night in a panic when she remembered yet another task or project they hadn't finished. But that had only happened a few times.

"I'm still not used to getting up so early to bake

everything." Brooke rubbed at her eyes under her sunglasses, yawning lightly. Her blonde hair was piled on her head in a messy bun.

Brooke had been baking all the delicious pastries for the inn's breakfast service, and the guests had loved them so far. It was hard to be unhappy if you were munching on a warm cinnamon scone and looking out onto the water. But in order for the guests to wake up to fresh-baked pastries, she had to arrive at the inn incredibly early to get everything in the oven.

"Well, you're getting it all done in time, which is good."

"Gosh, barely. I nearly burned some muffins this morning, but I caught them just in time. I'm glad it all turned out okay." Brooke lifted her sunglasses, resting them on the top of her head as she glanced over at Angela. "Speaking of turning out okay, how are things with Scott? I didn't really see him at the party, but I wasn't sure if we kept missing each other or not."

Angela bit her bottom lip. She hadn't told Brooke anything about what happened with her soon-to-be ex-husband, Scott. With everything going on at the inn on the day of the grand opening celebration, Angela had only taken a few minutes to gather herself from the emotional blow of her marriage definitively ending before going back to her preparations for the party.

"It's over for real now. Not just a separation—we're going to be getting a divorce. He kept promising to do better, but he had his chance, and he messed it up again." Angela grimaced. "I happened to see a message pop up on his phone, and I found out he was getting flirty texts from a coworker. Right in the middle of helping us prepare for the party."

"Ugh, seriously?" Brooke kicked a few pebbles down the beach. "When he was supposed to be showing you just how supportive and willing to change he was?"

"Right in the middle of it, yeah. So, I confronted him, and he tried to pass it off as nothing, even though it wasn't nothing. He claimed he wasn't encouraging her, but she had sent him over a dozen texts, and he wasn't exactly telling her to stop. I told him I was done and wanted to finish going through with the divorce. We talked for a bit longer, and then... he left before the party even started."

"Oh, no. I'm so sorry, Angie."

"Thanks." Angela let her gaze drift into the distance, taking in the rows of docks and the bobbing boats next to them. No matter how many times she talked about her marriage ending, it still felt a little surreal.

"I can't believe that happened while everything else was going on. You seemed so focused and put together at the party," Brooke said. "I would have been a crying mess."

"I was, for a second. I was sitting in the pantry bawling when Lydia found me and helped me pull myself back together."

Angela half-smiled at the memory, even though it was bittersweet. Lydia always seemed to know just what to say to get her back on her feet. She was so glad she had bumped into her childhood best friend in downtown Marigold that fateful day several months ago.

The two had fallen out of touch when they'd started their lives after college, jobs and husbands and kids pulling them in different directions. But they'd picked up with their friendship right where they had left off when they'd ended up in Marigold again at the same time. Lydia's support through all the anxieties of her relationship and opening the inn meant so much to Angela.

"Honestly? I would never dream of telling you what to do in your relationship or what decision to make for your family, but I think it's for the best,"

Brooke said. "You gave Scott a real chance to prove himself and be a better husband, which I really respect."

"You do?"

"Totally. I don't know if I could have done that nearly as gracefully as you did."

Angela relaxed a bit. She'd been so filled with self-doubt after discovering that Scott had cheated on her by sleeping with another woman. Opening the inn with Lydia had given her something to focus on, but when Scott had shown up on Marigold asking for another chance, Angela had felt torn between her old life and her new one. She had their six-year-old, Jake, to consider, and she'd wanted to do what was best for him, not just what was best for her. Hearing her sister's supportive words cemented the fact that she had done the right thing.

"Getting texts from that other woman right in the middle of his attempt to win you back makes it seem like he'd never change." Brooke shrugged. "That kind of man needs the thrill of being chased for his ego's sake, you know? That's not a winning recipe for a good partner."

"Definitely not."

Brooke was younger than Angela by seven years and single, but she still gave excellent advice and was a great sounding board. They had been apart for several years after Angela went off to college and started her life in Philly, and in that time Brooke had grown to be an amazing person to lean on.

But even with the support from her family and friends, the ache still sat in Angela's chest.

Her marriage was truly over, and since she had given Scott the chance to fix things, she would never have to wonder 'what if?' She'd made her choice and was sticking to it. No need to drag it out and torture herself, or more importantly, Jake, with endless back and forth.

But Jake was still the biggest hurdle she had to face. She had no idea how to explain what all of this divorce stuff meant to him—that she and his dad would no longer be together, and that he would only see Scott if he came to Marigold or if Jake went to Philadelphia. Jake had adjusted incredibly well to living on the island, making tons of friends and spending more time with his family than ever. She didn't want to ruin that with news that was sure to upset him.

Angela sighed and pushed those thoughts aside. She would think about all of that later.

"Anyway, what's done is done," she said, taking a

breath to clear her head. "Are you excited about the Summer Sand Festival?"

"Oh, yeah." Brooke grinned. "I always forget how much I love it until it's almost here. There are already so many more tourists in town."

"Yeah, Millie said the turnout is supposed to be bigger than ever." Lydia's aunt Millie seemed to have a hand in everything on the island. She was well-versed in every bit of town gossip and seemed to be friends with nearly everyone. "It's been so long since I've been to the festival."

"It felt huge last year." Brooke tugged on her long blonde ponytail absently, the way she always had when she was a little nervous. "I rented a booth at the farmer's market section of the festival. I think I'm going to make some beach themed cupcakes and other little treats. Since there are a lot of families, I'll probably go for cookies and brownies too."

"You did? Brooke, that's awesome!"

"Just for a day, though."

"But still, that's a big step."

Brooke's smile came back, brighter than ever. "It is. After seeing you and Lydia take the inn from what it once was to a fully operating business, I feel like I can take a few more steps toward making my baking an actual business too. Baby steps."

"You're already gathering a fan base at the inn, and it's only been a few days. I know you can do it."

Angela could hardly contain her excitement for Brooke, squeezing her sister's forearm a little. Opening the Beachside Inn was the most satisfying thing Angela had ever done in her professional life by far, and she knew that Brooke could truly find her purpose if she opened up her own bakery.

Some days, Angela woke up and could hardly believe she'd done something as risky as striking out on her own and opening a business with an old friend. Even though Brooke had mentioned something to this effect before, knowing that she'd inspired her sister to shoot for her dreams make Angela feel incredible. She had grown a lot in the past few months, in ways she was only now beginning to see.

"We should probably head back to the inn," she said, checking her watch. "There's a lot to do today."

Brooke nodded. "Good idea. It's getting a little late."

Back in Philly, Angela had always made her to-do list the night before, just so she could get things off her mind enough to sleep. But running an inn meant things constantly fluctuated. She had woken up this morning, taken a look at every pressing matter around her, and realized that only about half of those things were on the list she'd written not even eight hours before. It was a lot to juggle, especially since many of those to-dos were things she had to learn on the fly.

But at the same time, she was thrilled to have enough customers to warrant such a ridiculous to-do list. The Summer Sand Festival was the biggest event of the summer on Marigold, and tourists were everywhere, enjoying all the delicious food and small town New England charm the island had to offer. Even if the inn wasn't as nice and cozy as they had made it, they probably would have had *some* bookings just because of the high demand for accommodations on the island.

There were several other smaller events later in the season, like small music festivals or craft fairs, and people always wanted to get away from their hectic city lives and enjoy the beach whenever they had the chance. There were plenty of opportunities to book rooms. She felt even more confident about how the inn looked after all the compliments from people at the party, too, and she knew that the photos on their website were inviting enough to make people want to stay there.

But even as she had that thought, unwelcome

statistics of how most businesses fared in their first year floated into the front of her mind.

So many of them failed before they could even get off the ground. Now that they'd had their big grand opening, filled with people and warmth, she couldn't bear to imagine the place empty and lifeless the way it had been when they'd walked inside on their first day as the owners.

Angela looked at the inn in the distance as they headed back down the beach, hope and determination rising in her chest. They had kept the historic old place alive, pouring time, energy, and money into making it everything they'd dreamed of. They had done too much work for it to fail now.

Hopefully, they could keep the bookings rolling in over the summer and beyond.

CHAPTER TWO

Lydia's morning routine had shifted dramatically over the past six months. At the beginning of the year, she would get dressed and have coffee before heading off to her job at a travel agency, going through the motions of living. Every day had felt like it passed in a gray-tinged haze.

When she'd moved to Marigold Island and bought the inn with Angela, her mornings had become a flutter of excited activity nearly every day. There had been a number of new challenges to face during the renovations, whether it was caulking bathroom tiles by herself or figuring out the quirks of their online booking software.

Now that the inn was up and running, her mornings were equally as busy. Every day threw something new at her, and even though it was a lot to learn, and fast, she loved it.

Lydia double-checked that the last of Brooke's morning pastries were back in the kitchen along with the coffee—they were—before she settled behind the front desk. There was always so much admin work on top of all the work she had to do making sure the guests were happy. She glanced at the time on the computer. Angela and Brooke had gone out on their morning walk a while ago and were probably on their way back, to Lydia's relief.

She checked the inn's email and sorted through what was urgent and what wasn't. Thankfully, today, most things weren't urgent. There were some questions about the inn's availability, whether they had vegan pastries, what the pillows were stuffed with, and more things Lydia would never have imagined thinking about when booking a vacation.

"Good morning!"

A woman's voice pulled Lydia's focus away from the screen. It was one of their guests, a returning patron who had stayed at the inn several times before Lydia and Angela purchased it and re-opened it. Her name was Margaret, and she and her husband Joseph had stopped by the front desk to chat almost every day since they had arrived.

"Morning!" Lydia smiled and waved. "Are you two heading out for the day?"

"We are. We're finally going to visit that seafood restaurant you recommended, The Happy Crab. Your recommendation for lunch yesterday was stellar," Joseph said, putting a hand to his stomach. "If all the food in Marigold is this good, I'm not sure we'll be able to leave."

"Absolutely! It's grown so much since the last time we were here, but in a good way." Margaret put a hand on her husband's arm. "We have to get going, but have a good day, Lydia."

"You too."

The short conversation made Lydia smile as she worked through the initial items on her to-do list. She liked the way guests seemed to feel at home at the inn, as if they were a part of the community on the island.

"Excuse me?" Another voice, much less friendly this time, made Lydia look up a few minutes later. It was a woman, probably a few years older than Lydia, and she was clearly not pleased. "Can I get some help?"

"Yes, of course." Lydia gave the woman a pleasant smile. "What can I do for you?"

"The water pressure in my room is terrible. It's

like trying to rinse off using a weak hose. I could hardly shower this morning. It's a miracle I was able to rinse out my shampoo." The woman frowned. She had far more frown lines than smile lines. "Can you do something about it?"

Lydia had come across customers like this as a travel agent from time to time—the *can't please 'ems*, as she and her colleagues had called them. If they were booked on an incredible vacation throughout Europe, as they requested, they would make a fuss about having to take so many trains and flights. If they came in asking for a warm place to get away for the winter, they would huff and say the suggested location was *way* too hot.

Nothing could totally satisfy them, and even if things *could* please them, they would find the smallest inconvenience and blow it up into a massive problem. Lydia steeled her nerves and took a breath. When she'd been working for someone else, she could brush off criticism pretty easily. But now that she was the one who had painstakingly chosen each shower head, the woman's words cut a bit deeper than they would have otherwise.

"I'm sorry to hear that," Lydia told her, sounding as apologetic as she could. "I can take a look at it."

"When will you take a look?"

Lydia had no idea when she would have a moment. And hadn't the woman just said that she'd been able to take a shower? Was she planning on taking another in the next hour or two?

"No later than three."

The woman mulled that over, her lips turning downward, then nodded. "Okay, fine."

"Is there anything else I can help you with?"

The cranky guest sighed heavily. "No, nothing you can fix. It's just... how it is at places like this. I should've known what to expect."

Lydia bit the inside of her cheek as the woman walked away, making sure no sign of her irritation was visible on her face. "Take care!"

The woman just grunted in response, making Lydia heave a sigh of her own and grimace. She was running an inn, and people could be particular—that woman wouldn't be the last guest to complain about something small, so Lydia would have to get used to it stinging more than it had at her old job. Hopefully, people like this dour woman would be few and far between.

But still, what had she meant by "places like this"?

Lydia sat back in her seat, doubt creeping up her spine. They had worked incredibly hard on the inn, and she knew a lot about the competing businesses on the island from the research she'd done as they prepared to open. The Beachside Inn had maintained its original charm with some modern updates, including the bathrooms. Brooke's baked goods were a hit, and there was always someone around to help a guest in need.

Were they not measuring up? She wracked her brain, trying to think about what could possibly be tweaked after months of renovations.

When her cell phone rang, it startled her out of her thoughts, making her jump. She glanced at the screen to see that it was flashing her daughter's name. Holly was traveling abroad in Europe for the summer, and with the time difference, it was probably around dinner time for her.

Lydia put the "Back in Five Minutes" sign on the desk and ducked into the kitchen to answer. Even though the lobby was empty, she didn't want to risk guests seeing her chatting away. And she could pick up a leftover scone from the array of breakfast pastries.

"Hi, Mom!" Holly trilled when Lydia answered.

"Hey, Hols. What are you up to?"

"We're about to go out to watch some independent film, and then we're all going out to dinner. I just wanted to say hi while I had a free moment." Holly chuckled. "Everyone has dinner so late here, but I've gotten used to it."

"Are you still in Italy?" Lydia leaned up against the table and took a bite of a scone. "Or are you back in Spain?"

"We're in Spain. We just got back last night. I used to think people were exaggerating when they said Italian food is so much better there, but Mom. This pasta was *so incredible.*"

Lydia laughed. "That good, huh?"

"The best. I can't even believe it. And the people are so nice too. This little old lady saw that my friends and I were lost on our way to a restaurant and called her son on the phone—he could speak English fluently—to tell us how to find it." Lydia heard the springs on Holly's bed squeak as she sat. "I'm so glad she did. My Spanish has gotten way better already, but that couldn't get me around Italy, obviously."

Lydia could easily see Holly's smile in her mind. Even though her daughter was going on twenty years old, she still had the same unabashed smile she'd had when she was in the middle of something exciting as a little girl. And Lydia was excited for her too. She still couldn't believe how quickly Holly was growing up. Even though she missed her only child dearly, she knew Holly was happy, responsible, and independent. She couldn't ask for more than that.

"Oh, whoops—I didn't realize I was so short on time. We have to get going to make it to the movie on time."

"Okay, stay safe. And you're a smart girl, so make smart decisions."

"I will. I promise." Holly's eye roll was practically audible over the phone, but Lydia knew she would take her advice to heart. "Love you."

"Love you too. Bye."

Lydia ended the call and took a bigger bite of the scone she'd grabbed. Warm or cold, Brooke's scones were perfect. The cinnamon ones seemed to be guest favorites, but Lydia loved the blueberry ones the most. They got the fresh blueberries from a nearby farm, along with other fruits that Brooke put into all the pastries. It was a small detail, but Lydia knew that guests appreciated a truly local experience.

She swept the crumbs into the sink, grabbed her keys from the front desk, and headed upstairs to the difficult guest's room. She held her breath and knocked, then waited.

No answer.

"Hi, this is management. I'm here to check on your water pressure," Lydia called.

There was still no answer, to her relief. Even though she was in a good mood after her chat with Holly, she didn't want this guest's attitude to ruin it. Lydia unlocked the door and stepped inside, glancing around.

The cranky woman and her husband were in one of Lydia's favorite rooms. It had better views of the trees than it did of the water, but the light was gorgeous in the evening. Angela's choice of a sage green paint on the walls was perfect, even though Lydia wouldn't have thought to choose it. It caught the light perfectly and made the room feel both calming and uplifting.

The bathroom was equally nice. Angela had carried the sage green into that room too, but in a more subtle way. The two of them had painted the cabinet under the sink the same green as the walls in the bedroom itself and kept nearly everything else white and fresh. It felt like a spa.

Lydia stepped around a towel on the floor to get to the shower. She turned the knob to turn on the cold water, then the hot water, then both at the same time. It seemed entirely fine, at least to her. It wasn't going to double as a back massager, but it was adequate enough for someone to get a very nice shower—far from being a weak hose, as the woman had said.

Still, Lydia wanted to be thorough. She stepped out of the room and went back downstairs, briefly checking to see if any emails or calls had come in. None had, and the few guests who were mingling in the common area didn't need her attention. She stepped into the kitchen again, resisting what would have been her third scone of the day, and called Grant. He wasn't a plumber, but he knew enough about home repairs to help her decide if she needed to call one.

Even dialing his number gave her a giddy, butterflies-in-the-stomach feeling. After her husband Paul passed away a little over a year ago, Lydia hadn't been sure if she would ever find someone special again. His death had been devastating, but buying and re-opening the inn had helped her find her excitement for life again. Unexpectedly, Grant was a part of that excitement—he was the last person she had expected to fall for, but here they were.

They hadn't really discussed what was happening in their relationship, even though they both knew there were feelings developing between them. But that didn't stop Lydia's heart from beating faster whenever she thought of him.

"Hey." Grant answered after two rings, his deep voice filtering into her ear. "How's it going?"

"Oh, not too bad. Just dealing with a guest who's not exactly easy to please." Lydia glanced back at the scones and broke one in half. At least she wasn't committing to a *whole* one. "She came to the front desk complaining that the water pressure wasn't right, but when I went to test it myself, it seemed fine enough. Still, it's subjective, isn't it?"

"It is pretty subjective. If it seemed fine to you, it probably is, but I'm guessing you still want to address it?"

She smiled. "Yeah, I was just calling to see what I can do about it. Do I need a plumber, or is this a quick fix?"

"It's a pretty easy fix. There are shower heads that can increase the pressure, and a lot of them are easy to install," he said.

Some of the tension eased out of her shoulders. "Oh, good."

"But don't go running off to the hardware store," Grant added. "It was one complaint—no need to buy up every adjustable shower head on the island just to please someone who would probably turn up her nose at a shower head being silver instead of chrome."

"Is there a difference?" Lydia furrowed her brows, laughing.

"She'd probably find one." He chuckled along with her. "But seriously, Lydia. Don't let her get to you. If the shower head feels fine to you, you can trust your gut and try to make it up to her in another way."

Lydia nibbled on her half piece of scone, trying to take in Grant's words. She knew he was right. He wouldn't tell her something that wasn't true just to make her feel better. But still, it was hard to accept. All she could think about was the woman sighing and taking a dig at the inn, over and over again.

"You think I can?"

"Of course you can. You're doing an incredible job with the inn. This guest just seems impossible, and her opinion isn't an accurate reflection of all the hard work you've done."

"And all the hard work you've helped with," she pointed out with a smile. "That woman and her husband are staying in that sage green room we painted together."

"That's one of the best rooms in the whole place."

"I know, right?" Lydia ran a hand through her brunette hair, smoothing down the errant strands.

"Anyway, I should get back to the front desk. See you later?"

"Definitely. Have a good day."

Tucking her phone back into her pocket, she once again swept a few stray crumbs off her fingertips before heading back to take up her spot behind the front desk.

She had called Grant for his opinion on plumbing and had come away feeling both soothed and worried. She wanted the inn to succeed and to make it everything she and Angela had dreamed of, but it could only do that if they kept the place booked up with happy guests. Hopefully Grant was right about it all.

She wasn't sure what she'd do if they failed.

CHAPTER THREE

Patrick's house had never looked this put together in the entire time he'd lived in it. Usually, there were books strewn about on every available surface, stray pieces of mail on the counter, dishes piled in the sink and jackets carelessly tossed over the backs of chairs in every room.

Now, it looked like something out of a magazine. Jennifer Lowry, his real estate agent, had helped him stage it for potential buyers. Now all of his furniture was rearranged, and a few pieces of art that he'd had in storage were prominently on display. It wasn't cluttered either, and the flow from room to room made much more sense. Jennifer had even put vanilla scent diffusers throughout the house to make it smell inviting.

"It looks great," Patrick told her, turning around in his entryway one more time. "I can't believe how polished it seems. It's almost like a different house."

"It's a beautiful home, so it didn't take much to bring out its best qualities." Jennifer smiled, her high heels clicking across the hardwood as she walked. "It should sell even faster with it staged like this. It's in a great location."

Patrick nodded, running his fingers along a little hutch that had been tucked into the corner of his office before. It looked much better here in the entryway.

"And I've found a few potential houses for you to look at. They're also great finds." Jennifer adjusted a piece of art on the wall. "So hopefully you'll have an official home to settle into soon."

"Yeah, hopefully."

Patrick hadn't wanted to wait to move out of his house. He wanted a fresh start as soon as he could, and a new, smaller place would be a perfect first step into his new life as a single man.

His separation and upcoming divorce from his wife, Aubrey, had been as amicable as a divorce can be. They were going to give each other space for a while but still wanted to be friends eventually. There wasn't a massive blow-up that had caused them to end their marriage, either. They were like two lines, drawn side by side. At first, it had looked like they were moving in parallel, even though they were aimed in slightly different directions—differences so small that they could hardly notice them. But the longer the lines got, the less parallel they looked. After a while, the two of them just couldn't bridge the gap anymore.

In some ways, it made sense to Patrick. They'd both grown up on Marigold and had fallen in love in high school, and now they were in their late thirties. In the intervening years, they had become completely different people. Back then, they'd been on the same exact page. They'd gone to the same college, waited to get married until after graduation, and moved back to Marigold Island not long after. Year after year, Patrick had settled into Marigold's slower pace with ease, but that same slow pace had chafed against Aubrey's desire for a faster, more exciting city life.

Patrick tucked his hands into his pockets, looking at the piece of art that Jennifer had just adjusted. Aubrey had bought it on an anniversary trip they'd taken to New York City. She had loved every minute of being there—the people, the food, the constant bustle. He had liked it... if he could sneak in a nap before they went out at night.

The subways were crowded—when they actually came on time—and if they managed to grab a cab, they sat in traffic for what felt like hours. Even walking down the street meant running into strangers, weaving around outdoor dining spaces or dealing with construction noises. It was all so overwhelming after a while. Sometimes he just wanted some quiet. He couldn't imagine living like that all day, every day.

Now Aubrey was moving to Boston, which she liked even more than New York City, and had gotten a great job. He hoped that she could live the life she'd always wanted to lead.

"Thank you for everything," Patrick said to Jennifer. "I don't know if I could have done all this on my own."

"No problem at all. That's what I'm here for! I promise everything will go smoothly," she assured him. "I recently sold a home not too far from here, and it was a very easy sale."

"That's a relief. Buying this house was the definition of rough."

He and Aubrey had gotten into a bidding war with another interested buyer, which they had luckily won. Thanks to a hefty advance from his publisher, they'd been able to afford to go a little over budget. Neither of them had regretted it. The house had been a perfect fit, and they'd made a lot of great memories here.

"Selling and buying homes can be so, so stressful." Jennifer's light brown eyes shone with understanding. "If you need anything, just let me know, okay?"

"Yeah, will do."

He let her out the front door and turned to take one more look at the staged home. Things were going to be fine—better, even.

He went upstairs and grabbed his suitcases. Most of his things were in storage, but he had the essentials: clothing, toiletries, books, and his laptop. More importantly, he knew where he could stay. He tucked his bags into his trunk and drove off, feeling more hopeful than he had in a while.

Angela had gotten used to the flow of guests coming in and out throughout the afternoon and had perfected her professional, polite smile and hello. But when Patrick walked in with an old beat up leather duffel bag on one shoulder and a big suitcase trailing behind him, she couldn't help but break her professional façade.

They had become friends almost by chance since Angela and Jake had moved to Marigold. The two of them had known each other in high school, though they hadn't been close friends at the time. He'd been a year ahead of her.

After she'd arrived back on Marigold earlier in the year, she'd kept running into him in town, and each time, he'd taken the time out of his day to chat with her. Running into him was always a nice surprise.

Oh, hey!" Angela said with a smile. "What's up? How are you?"

"Not bad." Patrick smiled back. "I'm glad *I'm* the one crossing paths with *you* instead of the other way for once. It feels like you always caught me in the middle of my biggest writer's blocks."

Angela laughed. "I know. I hope our chats helped get things moving again creatively. Well, the chats or the fresh air or the ice cream from the Sweet Creamery."

"It was all three, I think." Patrick looked around the lobby, nodding approvingly. "It's nice to see things up and running."

"You're looking for a room?" Angela glanced down at his luggage, which appeared to be absolutely stuffed with clothes. "For a while, based on your bags?"

"Yep." He shifted the strap on his shoulder as if to punctuate his point. "Is there an open one?"

"There is." Angela pulled up their booking software. "You mentioned needing a place to stay at the party, didn't you?"

"I did, but I wasn't sure when my house would be ready to go on the market," he said. "I just need somewhere to call a temporary home until it sells and I find a new place."

Angela nodded and found an available room for him. It was one of her favorites, although she adored every room. It faced the ocean and got great light at certain times of day, highlighting the blue of the walls. There was also a small desk in the corner with a great view, which was the perfect spot for Patrick to work on his next novel.

She had never tried to write anything longer than a short story in high school, but if she were a writer, she would have loved that spot. Just looking outside, seeing people walking in the distance and boats drifting in the beautiful water could stir anyone's imagination.

"Are you looking at smaller places?" Angela asked, clicking a few times to get to the right screen of the booking software.

"Yeah, I am. Since it's just me now, I don't need that much space—just enough room for a place to sleep and my office. And I just wanted a fresh start with the divorce and all."

He had told her about his divorce at their grand opening party. At the time, she had just barely been wrapping her head around the fact that things were officially over with Scott, so she hadn't said anything. But now, she had digested the idea a little more and felt like she understood Patrick more than ever. She had seen the visible shift in him from a constant simmering of tension under his skin to a new lightness to his step. Brooke had mentioned noticing a similar change in Angela too.

No matter how stressful divorce was, there was some relief in it too—in finally having made the decision and leaving behind all the doubt and second-guessing.

"I get that. I'm going through a divorce too, and being in a new environment has been so helpful in moving on." Angela handed him a form and a pen. "Can you fill this out for me?"

"Sure thing." He gave her a small smile as he

filled out his personal details for their system. Then he glanced up, his green eyes meeting hers. "I didn't know you were going through a divorce too."

"Yeah, it's somewhat recent. I'm still getting used to how much of a pain it can be in every way. I forgot how many things we did together when we were married, so getting things sorted out is hard. Then there are the lawyers and the things that we haven't touched in storage for years that we have to split up now."

"It really is a lot." He paused to write something down. "Everything from the books to the grocery shopping to annoying household admin stuff is all on me now. And I bet it's even harder on you with Jake."

Patrick's sympathetic glance was welcome, even though Angela hadn't anticipated feeling as comforted by it as she did. A lot of people had told her they were sorry, but it didn't feel like they understood her as much as Patrick did in that moment.

"It is, but in some ways it's easier." Angela took the clipboard and form back from Patrick when he pushed it toward her and put it down next to her keyboard. "Jake loves his new school and all of his new friends and teachers. Plus, all of my family is here, so I've had a lot of people to lean on. My ex and

I didn't end on the best of terms, so it's been helpful to have that support system."

"Ah, I'm really sorry."

"It's for the best. I would prefer this to having him look elsewhere over and over again right under my nose." Angela shrugged. The words were feeling more and more true and easy to admit as the days went by. "It's very freeing. I guess that's the word I'm looking for."

Patrick seemed to quickly put the pieces together and frowned, his eyes flashing with shock. The expression was so odd on him—he was so nice and friendly all the time, even when she saw him looking at his laptop in mild frustration from a distance. He must have truly been upset on her behalf to actually show it, and that knowledge warmed her from the inside.

"Wow, how awful." One of his hands closed into a slight fist on the front desk. "You don't deserve that. No one does."

"Thank you, Patrick." An email alert pulled her attention away from him, and she noticed the time. "Oh wow, I must be holding you up. I don't want to take up too much of your time. Let me take you up to your room."

Angela was glad that Patrick couldn't see the

embarrassed flush across her cheeks as they walked up the stairs to his room. They were friends, sure, but that didn't mean she should throw professionalism out the door all together. He needed a place to stay, not a chit-chat about his personal life, but the minutes had flown by before she knew it. He was just so easy to talk to.

"Here it is!" Angela opened the door to the suite. "The view from the desk is amazing, especially around sunset. "

"Oh, wow. This is perfect." Patrick's eyes lit up. "Did I tell you that I love to look out the window when I write?"

"I'm not sure, but I could've guessed with all the walks you take." Angela stepped aside so he could go in.

"Thank you." Patrick put his bags down. "I'll be working on brainstorming and drafting a new novel while the one I finished recently is with my editor, so I'll probably be looking out there often, wracking my brain for ideas all day and night."

"Well, I hope it helps you find inspiration." Angela gestured to the bedside table. "There's a small booklet that has details about the island, which you already know, but there's also information on the inn's breakfast and other activities. And I'll be at the front desk if you need anything."

"All right. I'll talk to you soon?"

"Yeah, of course." Angela rested her hand on the door frame. "Rest up, okay?"

"Will do."

Angela gently shut the door, releasing a breath. She wished she could talk longer, but she had an inn to run.

CHAPTER FOUR

Lydia had dug deep into her closet to find the perfect dress for the evening. It was sleeveless and teal, hugging her waist before flaring out around her hips. It wasn't too dressy, but it wasn't too casual. She hadn't even planned on buying it but hadn't been able to resist when she'd caught sight of it in the store, which was unusual for her—she wasn't one for impulse purchases. Holly had convinced her to try it on and insisted that she buy it "just in case."

Now, Lydia finally had a reason to wear it. Tonight was her first official date with Grant. Even though feelings had definitely developed between them, this was the first time they were going somewhere together with a purpose behind it.

She smiled to herself as she thought back to how Grant had asked her out.

As much as I enjoy painting furniture and patching drywall with you, I'd love to take you on a date that doesn't involve anything from the hardware store, he'd said.

Lydia smoothed her brown hair behind her ears and looked at herself in the mirror. At thirty-nine years old, she had some laugh lines settling in around her mouth and eyes, but she liked the way she looked. Although she rarely wore much makeup, tonight had seemed like a good excuse to put in a bit of extra effort. It had been so long since she'd gotten dressed up, and she'd forgotten that she enjoyed the process. She still looked like herself, but with a little extra sparkle.

She brushed a bit of extra powder across her forehead and put her makeup away. Now that she was closer to leaving, nervous butterflies appeared in her stomach. In many ways, she was glad that things were happening in this order—preferred it, even. She hadn't even been looking for a relationship before, and if Grant had asked her out when they'd first met, she probably would have said no.

His grumpy walls had been up back then, so things probably would have felt different anyway.

Their surprising connection was what had helped them get close despite their past heartbreaks. If she hadn't ended up talking to Grant as he'd fixed the leaking pipe under the kitchen sink in the innkeeper's residence that night, would they have ever broken down the walls they both had up?

Lydia took one more look at herself before leaving the innkeeper's residence and heading into the lobby of the inn. She rifled through her purse for nothing in particular, trying to burn off nervous energy as she waited. Soon, the front door opened and Grant walked in.

She felt her heart stutter a little in her chest. She was used to seeing him in t-shirts or, on cooler evenings, a flannel shirt with the sleeves rolled up, his wavy dark hair mussed. Now he was wearing a crisp white button-down and navy blue pants, clean-shaven with his hair tamed. She'd already known he was handsome, but she hadn't known he could look this amazing.

He smiled at her, and it made his whole face brighten. She wouldn't have believed he could smile like that when they'd first met. Especially not at her. But Grant had surprised her. Underneath his gruff exterior was a sweet, thoughtful man.

"You look beautiful," he said, taking her hand and giving it a squeeze.

"You look great too." She kissed him on the cheek. "Ready to eat?"

"Very ready. Let's get going."

Grant drove them to the boardwalk, to one of the seafood restaurants that Lydia hadn't been able to try yet, but had been wanting to for a while. She had mentioned it to Grant offhandedly weeks ago and couldn't believe he remembered that she was interested in going. The place was incredibly inviting, with massive open windows and tables set out on the boardwalk.

They were seated outside, giving them a stellar view of the water and the open space on the boardwalk where a jazz quartet was setting up. Lydia pored over the menu, which featured seafood dishes from around the world with a New England twist. Neither of them could decide on just one thing to get, so they chose a few of the smaller plates to split—classic crab cakes, a stew with freshly caught local fish poached in coconut milk with hot peppers, and crab-stuffed sole with vegetables.

They thanked the waiter after he took their order, leaving them be with a bread basket. They dug in, their hands brushing as they went for two pieces that were next to each other. They laughed and tore the pieces of bread apart.

"If the rest of this food is as good as the bread, then we're in for a treat," Lydia said. "Did you remember me mentioning this place, or was this a coincidence?"

"I remembered you mentioning it." Grant buttered his bread. "You've been so busy with the inn that I wanted to pick something special."

She smiled, the fluttery feeling in her stomach returning. "Thank you for taking me here."

He grinned back. "Of course."

The waiter returned with their wine, a crisp white that would complement their food perfectly.

"To the inn?" Grant lifted a brow, raising his glass.

"Sure, why not?"

They tapped their glasses together and sipped the wine, making sounds of appreciation. Lydia couldn't wait to taste it with the food.

"How are things going at the inn, by the way?" he asked.

"Hectic." She drew in a breath, relishing the ocean air. "I don't regret opening the inn one bit. But there's definitely been a learning curve. It feels like every day is a whole slew of new problems I haven't even thought of before. There's the normal stuff like guests running out of toilet paper at odd hours, then the weird stuff."

"What kind of weird stuff? Nothing dangerous, right?"

"Oh no, not dangerous. Just strange, like this sweet older woman who asked me to shoo away a seagull that was sitting on her windowsill. At first, I was wondering why she was so nervous and why she was asking me to help, but then I saw it—and, wow. Seagulls look massive up close, as it turns out. It was almost like it was staring at her with its creepy little eyes."

"Seriously?" Grant snorted, then laughed. "Why was it there?"

"Who knows? I kept trying to shoo it away through the window, but it wouldn't leave!" Lydia started laughing again too. "I didn't want to open the window and make things worse. Eventually it flew away. And then on top of that, our booking system had some sort of glitch that same day, so Angela and I spent a panicked hour with their tech support on the line trying to get all of our bookings back. Thankfully, they were able to restore them and we figured out the root of the issue so it won't happen again."

"I've been there." He shook his head. "With the technology part, not the seagull."

Lydia scrunched up her nose. "Yeah?"

Grant owned a successful landscaping business, so he was always the perfect soundboard for all the things she was dealing with at the inn.

"Yup. We switched over from pen and paper booking to online booking for home landscaping work a while back—the day-to-day stuff like lawn trimmings and planting—and we lost two months' worth of bookings. We didn't get them back."

"Ouch."

"Yeah." He grimaced. "But we learned from it. It seems like you two are learning quickly, way faster than I ever did." He seemed genuinely impressed, which made a flush of pride rise up in her chest. "You guys are doing a great job."

"It doesn't feel like it some days."

"It'll smooth out, I promise."

Their food came a short while later, and they continued to chat about the inn and his landscaping business in between delicious mouthfuls. It tasted like the chef must have pulled all the seafood from the sea just minutes before cooking it, and every dish perfectly merged New England with other world cuisines, as the menu had promised.

Lydia finished her wine, which was just as delicious with the food as she had hoped it would be, and excused herself to the restroom. As she washed her hands, she looked at herself in the mirror. Her cheeks were a little flushed from the wine and the slight chill in the air, and her lipstick was long gone, but her eyes were bright with happiness.

She almost didn't recognize herself compared to the person she'd been even a few months ago, and she knew Paul would have been glad to see the joyful light gleaming in her eyes.

* * *

I'm the luckiest man in this restaurant, aren't I? Grant thought as he watched Lydia walk back from the restroom.

She was a beautiful woman on any day, but something about her smile, trained on him, and the way the evening light caught on her green eyes made her especially gorgeous in this moment. Her long brown hair cascaded down her shoulders, playing nicely off the teal of her perfectly fitting dress, and she had reapplied the lipstick that he liked so much.

"Oh, they dropped off the dessert menu?" she asked as she sat back down.

"They did." Grant turned the menu at an angle so they could both read it.

"I was full until I read this. But I think I could find a little more room for something sweet," Lydia said with a chuckle. "All of it looks so good. Want to split some things again?"

"Definitely." He skimmed the menu, pursing his lips. "How about the blackberry tart and maybe the chocolate one too? The waiter said they were small enough to share."

"Those sound perfect. Should we be daring and throw in the poached summer fruits too?"

"Works for me."

Grant caught the waiter's eye and ordered for them, adding coffee for both of them as well.

"I almost couldn't decide between the poached summer fruits and the panna cotta." She sighed contentedly, tucking her hair behind her ears. "I guess we'll have to come back to try them all."

"I'm glad you didn't pick the panna cotta," Grant said, barely suppressing a shudder. "I'm not the biggest fan."

"Really? Why?"

Lydia's curious expression was one of his favorites—her eyes widened and she cocked her head to the side a little bit, which he didn't think she did consciously.

"The texture. I can't handle smooth foods." He ran a hand through his hair, mussing up the careful style he'd created. "I've always disliked them, for as long as I can remember."

"Smooth foods?" Her brows furrowed. Clearly, it was the last explanation she would have expected him to give. "Like pudding and ice cream and things like that?"

"Yup. It has to have some sort of crunchy topping, and even then, I don't know. It can be a little iffy. Plain chocolate or vanilla ice cream... I can hardly stand the thought of it on my tongue."

Lydia burst into one of her big laughs, making Grant smile. He knew she wasn't judging him, though he would have understood if she did. It was a strange thing to be picky about. But that wasn't Lydia's style, which was one of Grant's favorite things about her. She accepted him as he was, down to the littlest details, especially as they got to know each other more.

"So you don't like the Sweet Creamery, then?" Lydia looked mildly horrified as she asked. Grant knew that she loved the place.

"They're the exception. The flavor is so good that

nice chunks of cookie or chocolate chips or nuts can save it," he said. "The mint chocolate chip is my go-to."

"Mint chocolate chip?" Lydia's look of shock dissolved into an amused grin. "That's it. I can't even handle that thought. Mint chip is the worst flavor of ice cream, no matter where it's from."

They both laughed and continued to banter back and forth about ice cream, their favorite foods, and anything else that came to mind, all the way through dessert. The desserts they'd chosen were the perfect ending to the meal, light but flavorful. As they sipped their coffee, the jazz band that they'd seen earlier finally started playing. People drifted over to an open spot under twinkling fairy lights and danced to the upbeat rhythm.

Grant stood and extended his hand to Lydia. "Want to dance?"

She took his hand, a pleased but surprised smile stealing across her face. "I didn't know you could dance."

"I have a few tricks up my sleeve. Nothing too fancy, though, so don't get your hopes up." He grinned, happy to have surprised her.

They found an open spot on the dance floor and fell into the rhythm of the music easily. He showed off his best moves, giving her a few twirls and even a dip, which made her smile so broadly that he was tempted to do it again right away. He wasn't going to win any contests, but he was a decent dancer. Good enough to impress Lydia, anyway, and that was all that mattered.

The music slowed down eventually, and he pulled her into his arms. She fit perfectly, the top of her head settling under his nose since she was wearing low heels.

Lydia looked up at him, her eyes warm and open. He leaned down and placed a gentle kiss to her lips. She sighed softly after they broke apart, dropping her head to rest it on his shoulder. He inhaled the pleasant floral scent of her shampoo and drew her a little closer.

He didn't want to be anywhere else in the world but here.

CHAPTER FIVE

Angela hid her relief when she saw the surly water pressure guest—or Water Pressure Lady, as she had started to call her in her head—walk downstairs, packed bags in hand and her husband trailing behind her.

Finally, she was checking out. Even though they wanted guests, Angela was happy to see her go.

Water Pressure Lady's complaint about the water pressure had only been the first in her many demands. Apparently, the water pressure had been a little *too* much after they'd quickly installed an adjustable head. The birds had been too loud in the morning, as if they had specifically targeted her and her husband out of spite. The almond milk with the morning coffee hadn't been specifically made to go into coffee, which "simply would not do" in her words. There hadn't been enough pillows, and the pillows that they'd had were too fluffy to find the right balance, so her neck ached.

Angela quickly took them through the checkout process, since yet another one of the woman's complaints was that everything was done too slowly at the Beachside Inn. It had been nerve-wracking trying to guess where she would strike next. Would it be Brooke's pastries? The thread-count on the sheets? The distance from Main Street—a whole ten minutes by foot?

"Thank you for coming. I hope you enjoyed your stay," Angela said, putting on a smile.

The woman shrugged. At least she wasn't rolling her eyes this time. "It was passable. Let's go, honey."

She turned, gesturing for her husband to follow. The man shot Angela a slightly apologetic look and headed out after his wife, carrying most of the bags. Angela waited until the front door had shut behind them to fully relax. She put the service bell on the desk in case anyone came in and headed back into the kitchen, where she found Brooke and Lydia chatting and drinking coffee.

"Water Pressure Lady is gone," Angela announced, finding a mug and pouring a cup of coffee for herself.

"Finally." Lydia blew out a breath, leaning against the counter. "It felt like she was here for a month."

"I know, right? Maybe because she was up at the crack of dawn and started complaining early." Angela sighed. "I know way more about the nuances of almond milk than I ever needed to, thanks to her."

Brooke pursed her lips, blowing on her coffee. "I mean, I guess it's good to know for the future? Maybe this almond milk creamer is a hot new thing that hasn't made it to Marigold yet."

"True. A small silver lining." Angela dumped enough sugar in her coffee to get her through the rest of the afternoon. "Apparently, we were 'passable' in her eyes."

Lydia winced. "Yikes."

"It sounds like she was trying to have a bad time, seriously. A person like that has to be dead set on being unhappy," Brooke commented. "Unless you could read her mind, there was nothing you could do to please her. She practically demanded that you get rid of all the birds in the trees like you could wave a magic wand and make it happen, for goodness' sake. Who even asks that?"

"I guess." Angela snorted, finally smiling for real. Brooke could be surprisingly spunky sometimes. "But our business lives and dies on reviews, especially since we're new. We need happy customers to spread the word, not women like her."

"True, but she's one of many. The others have seemed really happy with everything, birds and all. That's a good sign," Brooke pointed out.

Angela nodded, as did Lydia. It was so easy to focus on the one bad thing in the midst of a lot of good things. Brooke was right—they couldn't help someone who didn't want to be happy.

They chatted for another few minutes before Angela headed back behind the front desk. The day started to go by quickly, with multiple groups of guests asking for recommendations, checking in or out, or just stopping to say hello. Just when she thought she could take a breath, a courier arrived with an envelope for her.

She tore it open right away, an unsettling weight pressing down in her stomach. Her divorce papers. She'd known they were supposed to arrive soon, but she hadn't realized that day was today. Since Scott had stopped dragging his feet after she'd made it clear that things were seriously over, the divorce proceedings had been speeding ahead rapidly.

She sighed and skimmed the top page. It looked pretty standard, but she would still have to call Scott to confirm how they were going to split custody. At least their conversations were civil and productive, if not strangely formal for two people who had been together for over a decade.

"Mommy?" Jake said, popping his head out from behind one of the walls in the common area. He had a smudge of dirt on his cheek from playing out back. "Are you okay?"

Angela tried to smile. "Sort of. I have to talk to you about something. Let's go outside."

She found Lydia, who took over at the front desk. Then Angela and Jake settled on the steps of the back side of the porch. She had been dreading this moment, but it had to happen. He deserved to know, and she didn't want him to continue wondering what was wrong.

"Sweetheart, you know how Daddy has been living back in Philadelphia while we've been here, yeah?"

Jake nodded. "I miss him."

"I know." She ran a hand over his hair. "Your dad and I are splitting up, so he won't be moving here. We won't be married anymore. You'll be visiting him in Philadelphia for a while—we haven't figured out for how long, but we're figuring that out. And you'll live with me at other times."

Angela held her breath, watching Jake's expression shift from surprise to confusion to sadness. Tears welled up in his eyes, making her suppress her own. No matter how many times she had seen him get upset, it still cut her deeply.

"Is it because of me? Was I bad?" Jake asked, a few tears spilling over his cheeks.

"No, honey. Never. It's not your fault. We both love you so much, and even though we won't be married to each other, he's still your dad and I'm still your mom. That won't change." She brought Jake in for a hug, but he climbed into her lap instead, sniffling. "It's just that things weren't working out anymore between me and your dad."

Jake rubbed his eye with the back of his hand. "So I'll live in two places? Will I still get to see my friends?"

"Of course you will. You can see your friends from here and back in Philadelphia." She kept stroking his hair, pressing a kiss there. "A lot of things will be the same."

Jake sniffled a few more times and let Angela rub his back until he was steadier.

"Okay," he said.

"I love you, sweetheart. You're very brave." Angela gave him another kiss on the head. They talked for a while longer, and she made sure to answer any questions he had, trying to put him at ease. When he finally ran out of questions, she stood and helped him to his feet too. "I have to go back to work, but come get me if you need me."

Jake nodded, used to the routine by now. "I'm gonna go play with action figures."

"Okay, honey."

As he trotted off, Angela watched him, feeling a little bit of weight come off her shoulders. He wasn't done processing the situation, but at least now he knew what was happening.

Still, Angela felt unsettled as she flipped through the divorce papers and eventually got back to work. How would Jake feel about going between Marigold and the city? It was a big shift. What if Scott started seeing someone? How would Jake handle that? Would the woman be nice to him?

Since Lydia was watching the front desk, Angela

headed upstairs to turn over the room that Water Pressure Lady and her husband had vacated. Her mind was so full of whirling thoughts that she wasn't paying much attention to where she was going. As she rounded a corner on the second floor, she nearly ran smack into Patrick.

* * *

"Whoa there." Patrick jerked to a stop, lightly grasping Angela by the shoulders so she wouldn't go toppling over the railing. "Sorry about that. I was a little zoned out."

"It's fine—I was too." Angela blinked, looking up at him.

He could clearly see that something was on her mind, something troubling. She usually walked around the inn with a pleasant look on her face, even if she was dealing with someone difficult like the woman a few doors down who had just checked out. Now Angela's mouth was tight and her brow was furrowed, even though she clearly tried to wipe the expression from her face before he noticed.

"You okay? What's wrong?" He dipped his head, letting go of her shoulders.

"Oh, um..." She looked a little confused that he

had asked, as if she wasn't expecting that kind of question from him. "It's no big deal, really."

"You sure? Because it looks like a big deal."

Angela shifted the linens in her arms and sighed. "I guess I must look pretty rough, huh?"

"Just a little distressed."

"Yeah." She bit her bottom lip. "I finally told Jake about the divorce since I got the papers today. He was upset, of course, but it seemed like he calmed down by the time we finished talking. I'm just not sure how he'll be in the long run." She shifted the linens onto her hip. "Hold on, let me put these down in the room."

Patrick stepped aside, and she went into the room the cranky woman had just vacated. She reemerged a moment later, and they settled on the stairs between the first and second floors. Angela rested her elbows on her knees and ran her fingers through her hair.

"Sorry I keep unloading divorce stuff on you," she said, heaving a deep sigh.

"Don't worry about it. I wish I had talked to more people while I was doing the paperwork and whatnot." Patrick leaned back against the step behind them. "It helps."

"It does." She gave him a weak smile. "I'm just

stressing out about how I'm handling this with Jake. Did I tell him too much too soon? Or too late? Should I have waited to do it until after the paperwork was all finished?"

"It seems like you're handling it well. You're being really thoughtful about it instead of just letting your own feelings about your ex get in the way."

Angela leaned back too, mirroring his posture. "You think so? It's just so hard to tell because it's all so new. I feel like I should have broken it to him much more slowly."

"Well, you can only do your best. You clearly love him and wouldn't do anything that isn't in his best interests." Patrick shrugged. "And it's a hard situation any way you cut it. I can't even imagine what it's like to go through this with a kid in the mix."

Angela ran her hands down her dark jeans and let out a shaky breath. Patrick wasn't sure how much he was helping, but he wanted her to know just how strong she was for doing all of this. In comparison to *her* divorce, his was a cake walk. Splitting up your joined library was hardly a blip compared to splitting up time with your only child.

"I always wanted kids," he said quietly, looking at a big painting of the coast on the wall beside them.

"That's one of the reasons Aubrey and I weren't right for each other."

Angela looked up at him, a surprised expression on her face. "I didn't know that."

"Yeah." He ran a hand through his hair. "It wasn't a situation where she was unsure about whether she wanted them, then ultimately decided against it—I always knew and assumed it was the right thing for me as well. But then over the years I saw that she wanted an entirely different pace of life than Marigold has. It wasn't just about having kids or not having kids."

"I can understand that. I'm pretty much over the city life, but I can understand its appeal for other people."

"Yeah, same here. At the end of the day, I want to stay on Marigold. She has a new job in Boston, and she's really excited about it," Patrick said. "She would have loved our children if we'd had them, but deep down, she would have been even more unhappy. I don't think I would've been able to forgive myself if she'd decided to stay and raise a family with me because she felt like she had to, you know?"

Angela nodded, tucking her hair behind her ear. "It's a big job. I admire her for being honest about what she wanted in life, even though I'm sure it wasn't easy."

"I do too." Patrick looked back at Angela, noticing the flecks of gray in her blue eyes. They weren't sitting too close to each other, but he still felt the warmth from her arm near his. Had he moved closer without realizing it? "I'm glad I can stay here in Marigold. I don't think I could stand living anywhere else."

"Same. I'd forgotten how much I love it. I didn't really appreciate it much when I was growing up here. It was always about doing something exciting or new." Angela laughed a little. "Now I love just being able to breathe and take a walk without dodging trucks and dealing with other city stuff. And seeing my family more often. I never realized how much I was missing before."

"Yeah. We lived in Boston for a while, and it got old pretty fast. It was fun in college, especially with all the schools there, but then real life set in. The pace of it was too much for me, and I never realized how much I talked to my parents until I didn't have scheduled breaks to come see them a few times a year."

"Seriously. And trying to find an apartment that

was passable and in budget in Philly was a nightmare."

"Boston was the same, especially in the winter. Once, Aubrey's and my lease ended in the middle of February, and we had to move in a blizzard. And since we were on a budget, we were moving most of the stuff ourselves with our friends' help." He twisted his arm so Angela could see the big swooping scar just below his elbow. "I slipped on the ice and got a massive cut on something—probably some glass. I had to get a ton of stitches. I'm lucky it wasn't worse."

"Ouch." She lifted her hand, almost like she was going to touch his scar, but then she hesitated and put her hand back on her lap. "It makes you look a little tough, like you're one of the detectives from your books."

He laughed this time. "I don't think I'd ever want to be one of the characters I write. I put them through way too much."

Angela's smile broadened, and Patrick felt a little twinge of something he hadn't felt toward a woman in ages. It was more than just enjoying her company, which he definitely did. It was something almost intangible, a warmth that filled his chest when he spoke to her.

He pushed that thought aside. Her divorce wasn't even final yet, and it was way too soon to even think about another relationship. He hadn't been on a first date in over twenty years.

But still, that didn't change the simple, undeniable fact that he liked her.

CHAPTER SIX

Brooke tucked a paper grocery bag into the back seat of her car, feeling accomplished. After waking up early to start the pastries for the inn, which she was finally getting used to doing, she'd made a few amazing berry danishes on top of the regular daily pastries. They'd been a huge hit, and Brooke had decided to test one of her other new recipes on the guests later in the week.

But she was out of flour—she was always running out of flour these days—and needed real food that wasn't filled with sugar, so she'd slipped out to run her errands. Angela had texted her saying she and Lydia had the inn handled for now, so Brooke decided to take the scenic route back to her apartment.

She had lived on Marigold Island for most of her life, but she still enjoyed its natural beauty as if it was new to her. Cranking up her music and rolling her windows down, she turned onto a side road that passed by the waterfront. She knew she would never be able to live more than thirty minutes from the beach—she loved everything about it.

Brooke glanced out at the land along the road, which had a gorgeous view of the water. It was the land that Hunter Reed had bought, although thankfully, he hadn't put a big hotel up on it. Hunter had tried, but the city council had rejected his request to re-zone the land. He'd been surprisingly okay with it, given that as a big Hollywood actor, he probably wasn't used to being turned down all that often.

Brooke liked to think that her scones, which he'd said were as good as ones he'd had in cities like New York and Paris, had contributed to his good attitude.

"Speaking of Hunter..." Brooke murmured to herself when she spotted the dark-haired man down the road.

She turned down her music and heard him yelling something, angrily waving his arms around. Brooke sped up and pulled over, her heart pounding. Was someone out there in the water, trying to get back to shore? Drownings weren't unheard of in the area, especially since it was easy for people to drift out farther than they intended to go.

She ran toward him, wishing she had pulled her car a little closer. He was farther away than he looked.

"Hey! Is everything okay?" she shouted, startling Hunter as she neared him. "Is anyone hurt?"

His gray eyes went wide for a moment before something shifted in his expression. His cheeks actually flushed a little.

"Nothing's wrong. I was just running lines for a scene." He held up a script, which Brooke hadn't noticed from a distance. "I have an audition for a movie coming up."

"Oh. *Oh!*" Brooke laughed, putting her hand to her chest as if she could calm her pounding heart. "I thought something horrible had happened, like someone was literally dying. You were so into it."

"I tend to go all out even in practice. I never see a ton of people driving down this road, so I figured I was safe from prying eyes."

"If you're just practicing, why not do it at home?" Brooke asked. Her heart was still racing, leftover adrenaline rushing through her body.

"It's gorgeous out here, so why not?" He gestured

around. "I would be nuts to move all the way out here from LA and not soak in the scenery."

"But yelling in public?" Brooke rested a hand on her hip, trying not to feel mortified for overreacting. "You're fine with that?"

Hunter grinned, and it made her heart rate pick up a few beats again. "Technically, this is my property. It's just the edge of it. So I'm yelling within *sight* of the public."

Brooke's mouth dropped open a little in surprise before she smiled. She couldn't help it. There was just something about Hunter that was undeniably charming.

* * *

Seeing Brooke's face shift from panic to confusion to embarrassment, and finally to the self-deprecating smile she now wore made Hunter like her even more than he had the first few times he had met her. So many of the people in LA kept their barriers up and wouldn't dare run toward an acquaintance at full speed, yelling at him as if he were on fire. It would be too embarrassing for them, too *uncool*, even if it were an emergency.

Brooke was clearly a bit embarrassed, her cheeks

flushed from more than her sprint across the uneven terrain. But she was quickly recovering.

"Okay, fine—yelling within the sight of the public," she corrected herself, still smiling. Then she lifted a brow, curiosity gleaming in her eyes. "What's the movie about?"

"It's a period drama, emphasis on the drama. The stakes are pretty high, and it's all very emotional." Hunter glanced down at his rumpled script. "It's very, very, *very* loosely based on this wealthy British lord's diaries in the late seventeen hundreds, and they've taken a lot of liberties with it."

"So it's all new? No one's really heard of it?"

"More or less, unless you're an academic who's studied that sort of thing." He shrugged. "It's a little more fun this way since people won't be as nit-picky about the details of the characters' lives."

"I bet. I get why people care, since the details matter, but sometimes it kind of sucks the fun out of it if someone talks about how the spoons are too modern or how some king's court wasn't actually set up in real life the way it was in the movie," Brooke agreed, chuckling. "What's happening in the script that's making you yell at the sea?"

"This scene is one of the most dramatic. My character's brother has just been killed in a duel, days before his wedding. So my character—his name is William—is angry about the fact that his brother never got to marry his true love and the fact that the duel was probably rigged against him."

"That seems like something you'd yell about back in the day. Or any day," she said.

"Yeah. William only yells in this one scene, though he does a lot of pacing and brooding while staring out onto his rainy estate." He smiled to himself a little. "That's the other scene I have to prepare. It's much more intimate and emotional once William has had the chance to process everything."

"That sounds really cool. I love a good period drama." Brooke squinted against the sunlight, looking between Hunter's script and his face with interest.

"Actually..." He smoothed the wrinkles out of his script. "Are you busy? Would you be willing to run lines with me? You can play Elizabeth, William's sister, and I'll read for William, of course. It's not the final script, but it's enough for me to audition with."

"I have time, yeah. But... run lines?" Brooke looked back at her car. "With you? I'm a terrible actress. I couldn't even say my one line playing a cow in a school play."

"You don't have to be good—I just need to

remember the timing and my lines." He handed her the script. "Here. This is the calmer scene, don't worry."

A dimple appeared in Brooke's cheek as she looked down at the paper. "Oof. You're going to regret this."

"I promise you I won't. Start where the yellow highlighter is."

Brooke found the spot and took a breath. "William, please. You can't go on like this."

"But I *can* go on, Elizabeth," Hunter said, adding a ridiculous amount of emotion into it on a whim. He barely managed to keep himself from laughing. "Our dear brother cannot. He will never see his bride again. Not until she joins him in death."

Brooke froze, her fingers on the page, clearly not catching on to Hunter's joke yet. She managed to hold in her shock at Hunter's over-the-top delivery, biting her lip as if to hold in a laugh as she continued.

"But we can't just leave our lives behind to stew in grief. His widow... well, his betrothed... she has nowhere to go. You have to manage the estate and help Mother," she said, her voice a bit stilted and strained.

She was trying, and he appreciated her for it, but

she hadn't been wrong about her acting abilities. Then again, he wasn't looking good at the moment either—although that was on purpose. They read several more lines of dialogue, and Hunter's delivery grew more melodramatic and over-the-top with each word.

"Let our family weep. I will not rest until I prove, once and for all, that my brother died a wrongful death." Hunter looked out onto the sea as he finished, lifting his arms into the air dramatically. "It was his dying wish. His dying wish!"

There was a long, uncomfortable pause as his voice echoed off the trees. Brooke stared at Hunter, looking utterly lost. Whether she was confused because he had thrown in that extra 'dying wish' that wasn't in the script or because he had given a horribly over the top performance, he wasn't sure.

He broke into a grin and eventually couldn't contain himself anymore. He started to crack up. Brooke quickly connected the dots and let out a big snort as she realized he'd been acting terribly on purpose. The snort grew into a belly laugh, and she tipped her head back, her blonde hair blowing in the breeze.

"I can't believe I got away with that," Hunter

said, resting a hand on his stomach as his laughter died down.

"I can't believe you tricked me. I kept thinking, 'maybe it's just his process to get all the drama out first? Maybe he's planning dial it down later?'" Brooke dabbed at her eyes, pulling her giggles under control. "Thank goodness. You had me worried."

"I'm sorry. I couldn't resist." He straightened back up, shaking his shoulders a little to loosen them. "Let's try it again. I promise I'll be good."

"Okay." She took a deep breath and straightened too. "William, please..."

Hunter slipped into the part easily now that he had gotten the joke out of his system. He had very little in common with William on the outside, but he could relate to the despair and the character's strong will to make things right. It was exactly the kind of role that he wanted these days—something that was a bit different, but not so different that people would wonder why he was cast, and not the same "handsome and tough hero" thing he had done over and over again.

In his years doing big movies, he had started to find the work a bit stale. Everything was rushed, the characters started to run together, and it felt like no one really *acted*. This role, even though it was a bit of a change for him, made him remember why he loved his chosen career.

Brooke read the lines, and this time the silence after they finished was a good one. She looked at him, clearly impressed with his performance. Over the years, plenty of producers and film executives had oohed and ahhed about his work, but most of them hadn't seemed like they truly meant it. To them, it was just part of being in Hollywood. Famous actor? Of course, act impressed. He knew of some actors who would get upset if people *didn't* fawn all over them, even if they were just getting lunch.

But Brooke seemed genuinely in awe of him, and it made his face grow a bit warm.

"That was... wow. That was really amazing," Brooke said, her eyes lighting up. "You're an incredible actor, Hunter. I'm sure you've heard that loads of times, but it's true."

"Thank you." The more his cheeks flushed, the more embarrassed he got that his face was going red. "That means a lot."

And it really did. She was right. A lot of people had told him that he was a great actor. But somehow, hearing it from her meant a lot more than those passing comments.

"Mind if we run them again?" he asked. He

didn't want to linger on those thoughts much longer—she had to have noticed his flushed cheeks by now. "I think I can tweak some things in my performance and make it even better."

CHAPTER SEVEN

Lydia had known Water Pressure Lady's bad review was coming, but still, it hurt. The cranky woman had gone to all the major review sites and dropped two star reviews everywhere.

The review read: *My rating is more like one and a half stars, but I can't give a half star rating. One star is just because they gave me and my hubby a place to stay. The half star is for the view, which is acceptable. The rest? Major disappointment.*

Lydia sighed and sagged back in her seat at the front desk as she continued to read, feeling worse than she'd felt since they'd opened the inn. She could only take in the rest of the review in bits and pieces.

Water Pressure Lady complained that their breakfast didn't have any healthy options—besides the banana muffins Brooke had made after she complained. There was no added sugar in those, but it was too little too late. The water pressure, of course, was an issue. The rooms were too warm in the day and too cool at night. Everything felt too "home made," whatever that meant.

They'd done literally everything she'd asked, aside from magically making the birds stop singing, and had tried to do more. But in the end, it hadn't made any difference. The two star reviews stuck out, and knowing human nature, Lydia was certain that customers searching for a place to stay would almost always read the lowest reviews first and then skim the higher rated ones.

They couldn't tell the review sites to take them down, of course, so she and Angela would have to stare at the dark marks on their record for a while. And that was assuming that this review was a one-off. What they were bombarded with bad reviews later on?

"Hey, what's up?" Angela asked, rounding the corner with a fresh cup of coffee for each of them.

"The reviews from Water Pressure Lady are in. One and a half stars, though she rounded up a little." Lydia turned the computer screen toward Angela. "Thanks for the coffee."

"No problem." Angela sipped her hot drink as she took the other seat, her eyebrows furrowing deeper and deeper as she read. "This woman. Ugh."

"I know." Lydia took a long drink of her own coffee, which Angela had topped off with some of the barista-style almond milk Water Pressure Lady had asked for. It was delicious, to Lydia's dismay. She didn't want to admit that Water Pressure Lady had been right, at least in this case.

Angela squeezed her shoulder. "Hey, don't get too upset, okay? This is just a bump in the road."

"Do you think we could have done more, though? To maybe make her stay more enjoyable? I hate that she had a bad time, even if it seemed like she was determined to have one," Lydia murmured, tapping a finger on the rim of her coffee mug.

"Nope, I don't think there was anything we could have done. You did everything I would have done with her, and neither of us got anywhere."

"I guess so. But it's just so frustrating, since we can't reply just to tell everyone how difficult she really was. She's managed to sound reasonable in this review." Lydia sighed and leaned back in her seat again.

"This is stupid, but I was just thinking about how annoyingly good this fancy almond milk is,"

Angela said, pulling up their booking software as she took another drink of her coffee.

"I was literally thinking the same thing!" Lydia said with a laugh. "It's just water and almonds. How is it this good?"

Angela gasped, her eyes going wide. "That can't be real."

"What? You didn't know that almond milk was just water and almonds?"

"No, no." Angela gripped the edge of her desk. "We have a booking for Meredith Walters for next month. Look."

"You're kidding." Lydia looked at the screen and back at her friend. "This is huge."

She knew Meredith Walters well from her time as a travel agent. The woman was a well-known travel blogger and reviewed inns, hotels, and destinations all over the country and the world. She was incredibly honest without being rude, and people loved her practical but fun take on modern day travel. Many of Lydia's clients had come in asking for trips to wherever Meredith had just written about. Even Lydia had checked her blog when planning her own trips.

A review from her would be worth twenty of Water Pressure Lady's, especially if it was good. And the traffic on her posts alone would probably send a flood of new guests their way.

"At least she booked a month out," Lydia said. "We need to get ready."

"We really do." Angela scrounged around in the drawers until she found a pen and paper. "We have to make sure we blow all the other inns on Marigold out of the water."

"More than that—we have to stand out."

Lydia took a deep breath and looked at Meredith's name in their books. They had already succeeded to some degree just by getting the inn open, but she hoped they could handle this new test. Their business's success was riding on it.

* * *

After they realized that Meredith Walters was going to be staying at the inn, Angela and Lydia immediately started working to make their guests' experiences even better. Some people had given some helpful feedback in their positive reviews, and the two of them had dealt with a wide range of issues from the unpleasant guest and her complaints.

But there was still more to do, and the next

several days were consumed with small tasks and projects around the inn.

They started with the outside, adding a huge plastic owl on the roof to deter smaller birds from gathering near the building. They also asked Grant to trim back some of the bushes where birds congregated in the mornings, so there wouldn't be as much space for them to land and wake people up before dawn.

Then they worked on the inside. They added flower arrangements, changed up the fragrance diffusers to a different scent, updated the booklets with information about the inn and the island, and of course, addressed the water pressure among other things.

A week later, Angela tightened the joint on one of the brand new shower heads they had purchased and installed. Lydia had replaced the one in Water Pressure Lady's room already, and they had worked out a deal for the rest, buying several more to replace them in all the rooms. It was expensive, but it was the little things that turned an experience from good to great.

Angela put her wrench down and turned on the shower, adjusting the head so that the pressure went from hard to soft. She wouldn't have dreamed of replacing a shower head by herself even a year ago—all of her decorating jobs had contractors to do that sort of thing—but today, she had replaced three.

A satisfied grin tugged at her lips, and she shut the water off and rose to her feet, brushing her hands together in satisfaction.

"The shower heads are done," she announced as she walked into the kitchen a few moments later, tool bag in hand.

Brooke and Lydia looked up at her from their cutting boards. Several bowls of freshly cut fruit sat in front of them.

"Already? Wow." Brooke smiled. "Who knew you'd be so handy?"

"I know. I'm a little proud of myself." Angela washed her hands and wandered over to the prep table. "How's the fruit going?"

One of Water Pressure Lady's complaints had been that there weren't any healthy options for breakfast, so they'd decided to add fresh fruit with yogurt and the no-sugar-added banana muffins that Brooke had whipped up to their daily menu.

"It's trucking along." Lydia shrugged, chopping up some melon. "I'm glad berries are in season, because all we have to do is wash them."

"And they're not that expensive." Brooke popped

a raspberry into her mouth. "At least, right now. I'm not sure how it'll be when winter comes."

Angela opened the ceramic jar on the counter, hoping there were leftover scones. There was half of one, which was fine with her.

"Maybe we can go with another healthy option in the winter," she said with a thoughtful shrug. "We don't have to think about that for a while, though."

Dollar signs flashed in Angela's head as she spoke. They had good working relationships with a lot of businesses and vendors in town, but that didn't mean they got all of their products at a discount. Fruit was expensive, as were the fancier brands of milk and coffee that they'd started stocking. This wasn't exactly in their budget, but they were working hard to make improvements without spending too much. She only hoped that it would pay off.

"What else is on the updates to-do list?" Lydia asked.

Angela dug her phone from her pocket and pulled up her to-do list. They had checked off nearly all the to-dos that they could accomplish on their own.

"We're about eighty percent done with everything. I guess we have Water Pressure Lady to thank for all of this, really." She chuckled dryly, raising an eyebrow. "If she hadn't been so demanding and difficult, we probably wouldn't have changed a lot of these things—or at least, not right away. But they're good updates."

"Yeah, they are." Brooke pulled plastic wrap over the top of a bowl of berries so it would be ready for the next day. "You even handled the birds!"

"Well, we'll have to see if that actually works." Angela snorted as she popped a bit of scone into her mouth, thinking of the massive plastic owl that she'd bought from the hardware store. Jake had looked at it, completely confused, and asked if it was a toy for him.

"Your only other option is to make birds stop being birds, so you tried, at least." Brooke put the bowl into the fridge, blue eyes shining as she looked over at Angela. "Or we just set up a party spot for other owls to hang out."

Everyone laughed at the thought of a row of fluffy owls along the roof of the inn.

"At least owls don't wake you up with their singing at five thirty in the morning," Angela pointed out. "I'd take some gentle hooting over chirping any day."

"I guess we'll see how it goes tomorrow morning." Lydia wrapped up the rest of the fruit and handed it to Brooke. "Do you have that budget, Angie?"

"Yep." Angela looked around for her tablet and found it tucked next to a rolled-up apron. She pulled up their budget spreadsheet.

As Brooke puttered around, prepping things for the next day's breakfast service, Angela and Lydia looked at the raw numbers. They had stayed within their budget for the updates, which meant that they knew exactly how many bookings they needed to keep the inn going. It was an intimidating number, one that would have sent a previous version of Angela running away screaming.

But now she only felt mild anxiety mixed with a healthy amount of determination. She looked up at Lydia and found a similar expression on her face.

"It's a lot," her friend said. "We'll really have to hustle to get this many bookings in the next few months."

"I know." Angela took a deep breath. "But I know we can make it work."

CHAPTER EIGHT

The Summer Sand Festival had finally arrived, and Lydia couldn't have been more pleased at the timing. Since they'd found out that Meredith Walters was coming, she and Angela had been going non-stop, almost as busy as they had been when they'd first opened. Long day after long day had taken a toll on Lydia, so having a bit of time off was going to feel like taking off a pair of too-tight shoes after walking miles.

"I'm so excited for this. It's been ages since I've gone to one of these," Lydia said to Grant as they walked hand-in-hand to the festival.

It was a bit of a hike, but there were hardly any parking spaces available, with all the tourists gathered on the island for the excitement. Lydia didn't mind at all. She could have walked the length of the island with Grant, talking or just enjoying each other's company in the silence when it felt right.

"It was nice of Angela to watch the inn for you. Both of you need a break." Grant squeezed Lydia's hand.

"We're trading off, don't worry. I picked today because a lot of the kid oriented events are in the next few days. She and Jake are excited about those."

They reached the edge of the festivities, which were toward the edge of downtown. Everything from there down to the beach was a part of the festival. The streets were shut down and filled with booth after booth as far as she could see.

"Welcome to the Summer Sand Festival!" A young woman wearing a hot pink t-shirt with a Marigold Island logo on it greeted them from behind the first booth they came across. "We have maps this year since the festival has grown so much. Be sure to check out the sandcastle making contest at three-thirty—it's supposed to be amazing. Have fun!"

"Wow, this is a lot," Lydia murmured, unfolding the map. It showed all of Marigold and had labels for what areas housed which attractions. "Where do you want to go first?"

"The food? I could eat."

"Same here."

They made their way through the festival, keeping an eye out for things that they wanted to revisit. There was the artisan area, which had tons of colorful jewelry that Holly would have loved, and a stage where musical acts would provide live music throughout the day. They passed rows of games, rides, and other things that Jake would have a blast with, finally reaching the food section.

It was enormous, spreading out in a big field not too far from the beach, and packed. Picnic tables were clustered to their left, shaded by trees. The aroma alone made Lydia's stomach growl loudly enough for her and Grant to laugh.

"Let's take a lap and see what's available. There's too much to pick from," Lydia said, lacing her fingers with Grant's. She was used to his rough calluses at this point and liked the feeling of them against her softer skin. She ran her thumb along the back of his hand, enjoying this simple gesture of intimacy.

"Why do I get the feeling that we're going to end up splitting about five different things or taking more than one lap around this place?" Grant teased.

"Because that's what we always end up doing."

Lydia gently bumped him with her shoulder, grinning.

"What are you in the mood for?" he asked.

"Oh man, I have no idea." She looked at the rows and rows of vendors. "I'll see what speaks to me."

They walked around, taking note of what seemed delicious. There were the foods that Lydia had come to associate with Marigold—fresh seafood and hearty meals that left her feeling satiated down to her bones—as well as brand new things she had never tried before like sopes, which were thick tortillas topped with meats, cheeses, or vegetables, and Ethiopian food that smelled incredible

They did the rounds and decided to treat the experience like a multi-course meal, starting with a poke bowl, which they split as they looked over the map of the festival to see what they wanted to do. Since the poke bowl wasn't exactly the easiest thing to walk and eat, they picked up a few empanadas so they could explore a bit before getting their next "course." They decided on a few different flavors of empanadas—molé chicken, spicy pork, and shrimp—and shared them.

Their first stop after that was the artists' alley, which had all kinds of art for sale, from outdoor sculptures to paintings to pottery. There were also a few areas set up where people could watch the artists work on pieces live. Small groups of people were clustered around certain artists, who were busy at work or chatting with their audience.

"Wow, that's incredible." Grant gestured to a woman painting a little boy's portrait in bright watercolors a few feet away.

The boy was focused on her ice cream cone as she sat for the portrait, which the artist was re-creating with a few swoops of bright paint. The woman made it look simple, placing paint in what looked like haphazard places at first before adding little details that made it all come to life.

"It is. I wonder if they get stage fright working in front of people." Lydia took a bite of a pork empanada. It was just spicy enough for her taste—more heat than a quick burn on the front of her tongue. "I've never seen something like this, aside from caricature art."

"Maybe. I can hardly draw anything, so it's hard to put myself into a painter's shoes," Grant said with a smile. "I can't even win at Pictionary. I'll draw a dog and everyone will think I've drawn a horse."

Lydia laughed. "So you're telling me my secret plan to host a Pictionary party is a bad one?"

"Depends on how you want to play." Grant

nodded ahead of them and Lydia started walking next to him again. "It's a lot of fun if everyone is goofing off or equally as terrible as I am."

"That's how I've always played it too. It's not fun if everyone's taking it too seriously."

"We should do something like that soon." Grant took the now-empty empanada wrappers from Lydia and tossed them out, along with his.

"We should."

Lydia couldn't stop her smile from growing. The thought of spending time with both Grant and her closest friends and family felt natural at this point. He fit seamlessly into her life, whether it was at the inn or in the few moments of spare time she had every day. She wouldn't have thought it was possible to juggle all of her inn owner responsibilities with a new relationship, but Grant made it easy. He was never demanding and didn't put pressure on her, but he never let her doubt how much he enjoyed spending time with her either.

"Next course?" Lydia asked, patting her belly. She was beginning to feel a bit full, but not so stuffed that she couldn't enjoy a bit more delicious food.

Grant nodded. "Let's do it."

They wandered through the rest of the artists'

area before heading back toward the food, stopping by the many handmade jewelry booths clustered in one section. Lydia picked up some dangly earrings that she knew Holly would love and made a mental note of what Grant gravitated toward—simple, rustic watches and practical but beautiful boxes—just for future reference.

They enjoyed their second course of mini lobster rolls as they wandered past a series of small auctions for charity, and later on, they split a paper cone stuffed with hot, golden French fries paired with an herby dipping sauce. As they ate, they watched a team of people build a school of dolphins out of sand and a little water.

"I know the Sweet Creamery has a booth here. I'm pretty sure they do every summer. Want to make room for dessert?" Lydia asked after they'd finished their fries.

"I always do."

They held hands as they joined the long line for ice cream. The wait passed quickly, and soon Lydia had a waffle cone filled with lemon pound cake ice cream and Grant had a cup filled with his favorite mint chocolate chip.

"This is really hitting the spot." She nearly

groaned in satisfaction, licking a stray drop of melted ice cream off the side of her cone before taking a bite out of it. "It's getting warm out here."

"Better eat it before it gets away from you." Grant grabbed a napkin. "You've got some on your cheek—let me get it."

She stopped walking and let him wipe the ice cream off her face. He did it with such gentle care that she couldn't help but feel a flutter in her stomach.

"All gone?" she asked, looking up into Grant's deep brown eyes as warmth filled her.

"Yup." He nodded, his deep voice sending a pleasant shiver down her spine. "All gone."

* * *

Grant was glad that his melting ice cream was neatly confined to a cup and not dripping everywhere in a cone so that he could focus on how beautiful Lydia looked. Her brown hair had been developing golden highlights because of the sun, and little freckles had appeared across her cheeks. And her smile...

She looked so full of life and happy to be here.

"What, is there more ice cream on my face?" Lydia asked, blinking up at him.

"No, you're good now. I was just taking you in." He spotted a standing table for them to stop and finish their ice cream. Plus, there were even more napkins laid out on the table for festival-goers. They clearly weren't the only ones dealing with ice cream messes.

"Taking in the fact that I'm getting this ice cream everywhere like a toddler?" Lydia laughed, grabbing more napkins from the dispenser and wrapping them around the base of her cone.

"No, just you." He took the moment to kiss her, tasting the lemony sweetness of her ice cream on her lips. "You're beautiful."

As much as he liked kissing her, he liked the little smile that always appeared on her face afterward just as much. She was so strong and determined, but he liked that he got to see her sweet, vulnerable side too.

She went back to her ice cream, still looking pleased. He loved that he could make her feel good, and he'd meant every word he had said. She truly was one of the most gorgeous women he'd ever met.

After a few minutes, they finished their treats and washed their hands, then walked around a little while longer. They looped back through the artists' alley, then headed to the farmers' market section to pick up some treats for later. They even played a few games, shooting mini basketballs and throwing darts. Grant won a massive stuffed tiger, which he gave to a little boy who hadn't gotten enough points to get it.

The early afternoon brought even more people to the festival. Grant had lived on Marigold for years and had never noticed just how many people gravitated to it until moments like this. Then again, he hadn't been to the festival in a while. Last year, he'd only known it was happening because he had needed to pass through the crowd on his way to other places.

"I'm surprised at how much stuff there is here," Grant said, lacing his fingers in Lydia's the way she liked. "I heard several people say it's been growing, but I didn't expect it to be this huge."

"You haven't been to the festival before?"

"Not in any serious way. It's never been my scene, really, but I'm having a good time," he assured her.

Before his wife Annie had died, they had mostly stuck to quieter events like dinner or going out on the water. After her death, he'd avoided every social event he could. He'd always seen himself as more of an introvert than an extrovert. Crowds often exhausted him, but he felt the opposite here. He liked seeing other Marigold residents and visitors having fun, and he loved knowing that his small island home had so many different things going on.

"I'm glad! I'd hate it if I dragged you to something you hate to do."

He squeezed her hand. "Anything can be fun if you're with the right person."

"Careful there, you might lose your reputation as Marigold's most cantankerous man," Lydia teased, even as she blushed.

Grant chuckled. Even *he* could see how much more he laughed these days. His employees joked around with him about it too. He had never been mean in any sense, but he'd definitely been a bit grumpy a lot of the time.

Now, he whistled as he pulled up old landscaping and put down new, fresh flowers. He usually spent his lunch breaks at the inn with Lydia and went back to his business's office feeling refreshed and ready to take on the pile of emails he had. One of his long-time clients had even told him that he was looking more rested these days.

He was different.

Instead of pushing the world away and trying to shut the door, he was throwing that door wide open.

He glanced at Lydia, who was looking around

the festival with a gentle smile on her face. It was because of her—she had turned his whole life around in a way he didn't expect. But he was more than grateful for the change.

CHAPTER NINE

Brooke checked her inventory list for the hundredth time that day, glancing up at the crowds starting to trickle into the farmers' market area as she let out a nervous sigh. The second day of the Summer Sand Festival was going to be just as busy as the first. She hoped that things would run smoothly.

Even though the farmers' market was much different than the inn or a real bakery, it was a good test run for her to sell her treats to the public.

She had arrived way earlier than many of the other vendors, setting out an array of scones, muffins, danishes, and a few cookies since it was early. She had all the cupcakes, brownies, and other more indulgent treats at the ready for later in a cooler underneath her table.

Baking everything for the festival booth was one of the most chaotic things she had ever done, and she was grateful that she'd had access to the inn's kitchen. The thought of making all of this in her apartment's tiny kitchen by herself was a nightmare. Luckily, everyone had pitched in where they could. Angela had gotten some colorful cellophane and ribbons for the cookies, and Lydia had helped her double-check her inventory list. Even Jake had helped, tying ribbons around the plain ties that kept the little packets of cookies secure.

Brooke adjusted the basket of wrapped up scones again to get rid of some of her nervous energy—not that it helped.

"First time here?" The woman in the next booth over, who was selling goat's milk cheese, asked. Her name tag said Margie in big, handwritten letters.

"That obvious?" Brooke asked with a laugh. "Yeah, it is. I'm so nervous that I don't know what to do with myself. I've come to the farmers' market as a customer plenty of times and loved it, but I don't know what to expect as a vendor."

"It'll be great! We sell at the markets around here all the time. You get the hang of it fast, and time really flies when you're talking to people," Margie assured her. "And all of those baked goodies look delicious too."

"That's good to know." Brooke smiled, feeling a little more at ease. Margie was just the right person to be her booth neighbor with her warm, easy energy to counterbalance Brooke's nerves. "Thank you."

"No problem, honey." Margie smiled back. "Actually, can I be your first customer? I didn't get the chance to grab breakfast. What do you recommend?"

Brooke's smile turned into a grin. "It depends—do you want to go sweeter or more savory?"

"Savory, I think."

"Then I definitely recommend my gruyere and prosciutto scone. It's one of my favorites."

"Mmm. Sounds perfect!"

Brooke found the scone and gave it to the woman, tucking the payment into her cash box. She tried to busy herself so she wouldn't watch Margie as the woman took her first bites. Brooke's family was used to her staring them down as they tried her newest concoctions, but she doubted a stranger would appreciate it very much.

"Oh, this is amazing." Margie spoke around a mouthful, giving Brooke a thumbs up. "Thank you."

"I'm so glad you like it." Some of Brooke's nerves melted away, and she beamed at her neighbor.

Margie took another massive bite, holding up a hand in front of her mouth as she spoke. "I love it. I might have to grab another one of your wares later."

"I'll save something for you."

Margie laughed, quickly finishing up her scone as she hiked up the money belt that was situated around her hips. Her first customers had arrived, and so had Brooke's. They had overheard Margie's approval of the gruyere and prosciutto scone and got two for themselves.

The foot traffic picked up, sending more and more customers Brooke's way. Margie was right—it was surprisingly easy to learn the ropes of manning her own booth, even if she was a little overwhelmed at first. The scones were going fast, as were the muffins. Brooke could hardly keep up.

In a brief lull, Margie suggested that Brooke put out a sample plate, which she did, using some toothpicks and a plate that Margie offered her. The small bites of her pear pecan muffins disappeared in a flash, as did most of her supply of them after that. Once the afternoon rolled around, she put out the cupcakes decorated in bright frosting, which was like a beacon for kids. Thankfully, there were a lot of activities at the festival for the kids to burn off their sugar rushes.

Satisfaction filled Brooke, the warm feeling of it building inside her with each customer she served.

There were few things as satisfying as watching people bite into her baked goods and seeing their reaction. Especially the kids, who weren't generally known for their tact. Some of them even loved the more sophisticated treats, like her earl gray tea muffins, which was surprising.

When she hit another small lull in customers, she dug through her bag to pull out her phone. She wanted to make a note to test more recipes out on Jake to see what other things kids might be interested in.

"Ah, did everyone get to the scones before I could?"

A familiar voice drew her attention. Brooke whirled around so quickly that her pale blonde ponytail smacked her in the cheek.

Hunter Reed was standing in front of her booth with a smile, wearing sunglasses and a baseball hat. He blended in with everyone else, who were also shielding themselves from the sun, so no one gave him more than a passing glance. Even though Hunter had been on the island for a while, Brooke was still surprised that he knew who she was. She never would have dreamed of being even *acquaintances* with a well-known Hollywood actor.

"Oh, Hunter! Hi! Give me a second—there are more scones."

Slightly flustered, she put her phone away and pulled out more scones. She also restocked her "everything but the kitchen sink" cookies and her classic blondies.

"Wow, all of these look amazing." Hunter's striking gray eyes gleamed hungrily as he surveyed the pastries. "I'm tempted to buy up everything here after tasting your scones. I still think about them every time I get one from somewhere else, because the others never measure up."

"Oh, wow. Thank you." Brooke flushed, unable to keep a big grin off her face. "I mean, if you wanted to buy everything, I wouldn't object. But I'm guessing you can't plow through several dozen scones, cookies, lemon bars, brownies, and cupcakes all on your own, can you?"

"You'd be surprised." Hunter stepped a little closer, a half-smile curving his lips. He pulled off his sunglasses when he got under the shade of her booth. "I can have quite the appetite when it comes to baked goods. My sweet tooth is pretty legendary."

"Good thing you're here, then." Brooke rested her fingertips on the table. "What's your favorite kind of baked good, besides the scones?"

"Hm..." He glanced over everything again. "I honestly can't choose. What's your favorite?"

"Oh, no. I can't pick a favorite type of treat—they're all perfect to me." She chuckled. "I love everything I bake, but if I had to choose something from what's on this table right now, I'd pick the earl gray muffins, the 'everything but the kitchen sink' cookies, a lemon bar, and a maybe a vanilla bean cupcake if you want an extra sugar rush."

"What's this kitchen sink cookie?" he asked, scanning the table before finding it.

"It's one of my favorites. It's a mixture of different kinds of chocolate, pretzels, and toffee. It's a little salty and a little sweet," she told him. "I was actually going to put some out as a sample. Want the first one?"

"I can't say no to a free sample."

She cut up some cookies and poked them with toothpicks, extending the plate out to Hunter. He took one and popped it into his mouth, letting out an *mmm* of appreciation.

"No offense to your scones, but I think this is my new favorite." He grinned as he spoke.

"They won't be offended." Brooke took a sample for herself, unable to resist. "They still care about you."

"Thank goodness. I'd hate to think I hurt their feelings." Hunter made a face of exaggerated concern, letting her know he was joking. "I think I'll take everything you suggested—just one or two of each."

"Perfect."

She bagged up everything she had suggested for him and tucked it safely into a paper bag. He paid and took it, digging inside the bag right away for one of the big cookies.

He closed his eyes for a moment as he took a bite, patting his stomach. "This is why I had to buy so many. I'll be lucky if I have any pastries left by the time I leave the festival."

Brooke laughed again. Hunter's charming grin and relaxed demeanor immediately put her at ease, and it didn't hurt that he was such a big fan of her baked goods.

A young couple came up to the booth to check out the offerings, and Hunter stepped aside so they could see everything. "Thanks for the treats, Brooke. See you around?"

"Yeah, see you. And thanks!" She waved as he

put his sunglasses back on and disappeared into the crowd.

The next cluster of customers hadn't recognized him—or they *had* and just didn't care. Brooke wondered if Hunter was used to people paying a little less attention to him now that he was settling in on Marigold. He had been there for a while now, and most residents were aware that they had a famous actor living in their midst.

Brooke's kitchen sink cookies went quickly, as did the time. Before she knew it, her parents, Phoebe and Mitch, were walking up to her, hand-in-hand. They never missed the Summer Sand Festival, especially on the days when there were wine tastings later in the afternoon.

Phoebe was in a pale pink sun dress, and Mitch was in a short-sleeved button down of a coordinating color. Brooke doubted that they'd planned it, but it was cute anyway. Her parents were still deeply in love with each other, possibly even more than ever since they had both retired. They were living the life they had dreamed of after wrapping up their careers —relaxing on the beach, playing with their grandson, and finally getting around to all the projects and hobbies that they'd put off for years or even decades.

Brooke knew she was a little biased since they

were her parents, but she couldn't think of a more deserving couple. They had given back to their community their whole lives, and now they could enjoy the fruits of what they'd helped the island build.

"Hi, honey!" Phoebe grinned as they stepped up to the table at Brooke's booth. "How is it going?"

"It's going great!" Brooke moved around the table and gave each of them a hug. "The traffic seems to come and go in waves, but when it's busy, it's super busy."

"You got a great spot. We saw you right away." Mitch looked at Brooke's table. "Did everyone get my favorites yet?"

Brooke laughed and ducked under the table to get the two mini key lime pies she'd set aside. "Yup. But I saved some for you."

"Oh, thank goodness." Her dad took the pies, glancing around almost like he thought someone was going to swoop in and steal them. "I'm so excited for you, but I didn't want anyone to get to these before I could. I'm itching for more of these."

"Mitch, she's your daughter!" Phoebe playfully smacked his arm. "You're family. She could bake you the pies whenever you want."

"True, but she's on her own now. I can't walk

across the house and find her baking up a storm anymore."

"I'll be sure to bring some for you guys to keep in the freezer," Brooke said. "Just because I moved out doesn't mean you're cut off from the goodies."

Brooke had lived with her parents for a while after she'd graduated from college and begun figuring out what to do next. It had been a stressful time, so she'd done a lot of baking to soothe herself and distract from their questions about the direction she wanted to take with her life.

She loved her parents, but she was happy to have an apartment to call her own now, even if it was a quarter of the size of their house.

Their freezer was already stuffed with what treats she could freeze anyway, so she knew her dad was mostly joking about the pies. Well, the freezer had been full the last time she'd dropped by. It always seemed to clear out between her visits. Between their family dinners, visits with Jake, and gatherings with friends, her parents were spreading the word about her baking across the whole island.

"So everything is selling well?" Phoebe asked, looking hopeful. "It's so great that you're doing this."

"Yeah, things are really moving. I've already run out of some things, especially chocolate chip cookies." Brooke felt a little swell of pride in her chest. She couldn't have asked for the day to go any better.

"What's left? Can we buy a few things besides the pies?" Mitch asked.

"You guys don't have to buy anything, Dad. It's on the house." Brooke sorted through what was left and picked the things she knew were their favorites. "If you hadn't been my taste testers, I doubt I would have gotten this far with my baking."

"You're great at this, sweetheart. If we hadn't been your testers—and we'll still be your number ones, of course—anyone with taste buds would have been happy to do the job." Phoebe took the bag from Brooke, giving her daughter a fond look.

"Thanks, Mom."

"Good luck, hon. We've got to get going—we're meeting the Hendersons down by the beach."

"Thanks for stopping by." Brooke came around the table again and gave them each a firm hug. She really couldn't have started this without her family, and she wanted them to know how grateful she was. "Tell the Hendersons I said hi."

Her parents walked off, fading into the bustling crowd. Brooke sighed as fatigue finally began to set in. She had been on her feet all day, and even though she was used to getting up incredibly early these days, she usually wasn't "on" so much, or for so long. She considered herself somewhere between an introvert and an extrovert, but her inner introvert was now taking center stage.

She took a seat for a second, drinking a little water and nibbling on some crackers and goat's milk cheese that Margie had given her as a gift.

Before long, she got her second wind and stood back up, stretching a little. But just as she was about to put out some more samples, a commotion sprang up down the line of vendors. People gasped, and someone cried out in surprise.

Brooke leaned her head out of the booth to see what was going on and spotted a flash of pink on the ground.

Her heart nearly stopped. "Mom!"

The word was torn from her lips as her entire body seemed to go cold in a rush. She glanced quickly at Margie, who nodded in understanding, before running off toward her mother's collapsed form on the ground.

CHAPTER TEN

"Wow, look at that, Jake!" Angela said, pointing out one of the many sand sculptures dotting the beach. "It's a monster truck."

"Whoa!" Jake's eyes went wide. He was practically hopping with excitement at the sight of it. "How did they do that?"

"I don't know. Let's watch them finish it."

She took her son's hand and guided them through the clusters of people who'd gathered to watch the teams create sand sculptures. The artists sprayed some sand down with water before packing it onto the truck, carefully scraping away at it until it was in the shape they wanted. It was like a grown-up version of the sand castles that she and Jake sometimes put together—and that Jake quickly destroyed for fun.

"Slow down, sweetie."

She tugged on her son's hand a little, holding him back from skipping down the beach. He slowed down a tiny bit but kept skipping.

Angela knew that he was going to end up crashing hard that night, just because he had been so excited throughout the whole day. They had come to the Sand Festival earlier in the afternoon and hadn't stopped having fun since. There were so many games and activities that there was never a lull. They'd already hit the games section, winning a stuffed dog that was so big they couldn't even carry it around all day.

They'd put it in the car before visiting the balloon animal station, where Jake and Angela had made hats and dogs—which could be friends with the stuffed one they had put into the car, as Jake had suggested cheerfully.

After eating pizza for lunch, they'd watched a few of the skits that an acting troupe put on for the kids, then played even more games. Jake had devoured some cotton candy too, which made him more hyper than ever.

Angela was absolutely exhausted, but seeing the joy on Jake's face made it easier to push through. He was taking the divorce well, although he had been asking a few more questions since their talk. He'd been curious about how he would split his time between Marigold and Philadelphia—something she and Scott were still figuring out. He'd also wondered whether his dad was happy—which appeared to be the case, at least as much as the circumstances allowed.

She had answered each question he'd asked as well as she could. She'd also made an effort to keep their routine steady and to tell him that she loved him even more than usual. They had regular calls with Scott too.

Angela's phone buzzed in her purse, and she reached inside to check if it was important. It was Brooke, so she knew she should pick up. Brooke had said she might need help with her booth when they'd parted ways that morning.

"Hey, what's up?" Angela squinted against the bright sunlight, trailing after Jake.

"Are you and Jake here?" Brooke asked, and the sound of her voice made Angela's footsteps slow. There was panic in her tone. "Mom collapsed. We need to go to the hospital. The ambulance took her away."

"What?" Angela stopped entirely, putting a hand to her chest. Instead of her heart pounding, it felt like it had forgotten how to beat at all. Without waiting for Brooke to answer, Angela continued. "Okay. We'll go right now. Meet you there."

She stuffed her phone back into her bag and composed herself a little, taking Jake's hand.

"Sweetie, we have to go. Grammy's not feeling well, and we need to go to the hospital, okay?"

"Oh... Grammy's sick?" The little boy's expression fell.

"Yes. Let's go see her, okay? The doctors are taking care of her, just like they took care of your arm when you hurt it." She let out a shaky breath and guided him back to the car.

In some ways, Angela felt the same way she had when she'd discovered that Scott was cheating on her. One moment, she'd been living her life as usual, and the next, it had felt like she'd stepped into a hole in the ground that she hadn't seen. And she hadn't seen this coming either. She'd never thought her mother would end up in a situation like this.

Angela weaved through traffic on the way to the hospital, making the drive in less time than she ever had before. She found Brooke, her brother Travis, and their father sitting in the waiting room, all looking tense.

Jake ran over to his grandfather and climbed into his lap, throwing his arms around the older man's neck in a hug. Mitch hugged him back, his eyes going a little misty.

"How is she?" Angela asked, taking a seat. She wasn't sure if the sweat she felt was from the warmth outside or her anxiety, but either way, it cooled on her skin in the waiting room's air conditioner, making goose bumps dance over her arms.

"We don't know." Travis shook his head. He was off duty and out of uniform, wearing a t-shirt and shorts. "She hasn't been with them long. I was downtown eating a late lunch with my friends and got here right when they took her in."

"What happened?" Angela looked between Brooke and Mitch, who appeared pale under their summer tans.

"We were just walking to the beach after stopping by Brooke's booth," Mitch said, letting Jake settle on his lap. "We stopped to take a look at something, and she just went slack. Thankfully she was on the grass when it happened, but I think she might have bumped her head."

Angela chewed on her lower lip. "She fainted?"

"It seems like it." Brooke shook her head, raking her fingers through her hair. "She was totally fine just a few moments before—nothing seemed off at all. We were talking and laughing. She didn't seem tired or dizzy at all."

Angela sat back in her seat, feeling a little queasy. Her mother was getting older, yes, but she still seemed so youthful in a lot of ways. She was still very active, playing with Jake and going on long walks with her friends, and she ate fairly healthfully. What could be wrong?

Anxious possibilities rushed through her head. What if it was some sort of heart attack? What if Phoebe had gotten some injury that would affect her for the rest of her life? What if her life, and all of their lives by extension, had permanently changed course?

They sat in silence, fidgeting and getting lost in their own thoughts for what felt like hours. The freezing waiting room made it harder to relax, and the hum of the air conditioner sounded like a mosquito in her ear. It only made the wait even worse. She'd thought that waiting to hear how badly Jake's arm was hurt had been difficult, but this was even more terrifying. Jake's situation had just been a matter of how bad the break was, but there were a thousand different possibilities for her mom.

Eventually, a doctor came out to speak to them.

"Are you the Collins family?" he asked. He had kind eyes that made Angela feel a little more at ease.

"We are." Travis sat forward, clearing his throat.

The waiting room was mostly empty where they were, so the doctor sat down with them.

"I'm Doctor Chase, and I'm tending to Phoebe. She's doing all right, aside from a few scrapes from her fall. But she needs to undergo some tests just so we can rule out more serious things."

Everyone visibly relaxed, and Angela could feel the knot of tension in her stomach dissolve a little.

"What are you trying to rule out?" Brooke asked.

"As much as possible. The more we know, the better equipped we'll be to deal with whatever caused her fainting spell. But based on what I'm seeing now, I doubt it's anything deeply concerning. Her health up until this point has been very good, even for a woman her age." Doctor Chase smiled a little, his expression calm and compassionate. "We're going to take good care of her, okay? I'll be back with some of the more immediate results in a bit."

Everyone murmured a *thank you*, and Doctor

Chase left. Angela rubbed her damp hands along her skirt, wishing she could do something more to help.

Please, Mom. Please be okay.

* * *

Doctor Chase's calm bearing and his update had helped Travis relax a bit, but not much. That seemed to be the case for the rest of his family as well. They all still looked worried.

What if the results that Doctor Chase brought back next had bad news? How would they handle it?

Travis dealt with difficult things all the time as a police officer, but having a health issue hit this close to home and being so powerless to stop it was much more overwhelming. He loved his family dearly and couldn't even imagine family dinners or gatherings without his mother.

Travis twisted his fingers together, thoughts spinning through his mind.

He was single and wasn't looking to change that any time soon. At thirty-three, he figured he had a lot of time to find a nice woman and settle down. He had his career, which he loved, and his close friends, who were mostly single too.

But now, he was rethinking everything. He

wanted his parents to meet his eventual kids and spend time with them, just the way they did with Jake. He dreamed of family dinners that were so big that they had to sit outside at tables pushed together, his parents sitting at the head of the table.

The idea of that had felt so distant up until today. Now, he fought off thoughts of doing all of those things without his mother.

"Patrick?"

Angela's voice dragged Travis from his thoughts, confusion crossing her face as she stood.

He turned to see a tall man with brown hair rushing into the waiting room. Patrick Devlin.

"Hey." Patrick sounded a bit out of breath when he spoke. "Lydia told me what happened and said you might need some more support."

Angela's expression softened, though she was obviously still worried. "Oh, thank you. You didn't have to do this."

"Well, I've already spent time in a doctor's waiting room with you, so this isn't unprecedented." Patrick squeezed Angela's shoulder in a way that had Travis's eyebrows sneaking up.

Interesting, he thought.

He recognized Patrick. He had read one of his books and knew that they had gone to the same high school, although in different years. But Travis hadn't known that Patrick and Angela were friends—or possibly on the way to being more than that.

He couldn't quite be sure what was happening between them, but the way Patrick was a bit flushed and disheveled made it seem like he'd rushed right over to the hospital, abandoning whatever he'd been doing to come to Angela's side. That had to mean something.

Brooke stepped on Travis's foot, drawing his attention and making him wince. He looked at her, about to ask her what her problem was, but her expression told him to bite his tongue. She glanced at Angela and Patrick, who were talking about what had happened, then back at Travis, her expression loaded with meaning. She shook her head once.

Ah. Right. Things quickly clicked into place in Travis's head.

Brooke was subtly reminding him to not draw attention to the spark of chemistry between Patrick and Angela, and to let their older sister figure things out on her own.

It made sense. Angela was still finalizing her divorce, so even if this spark that he thought he saw was real, he doubted she would want to dive into another new relationship right away. It was too soon, and he knew Angela was still reeling a bit from the changes and upheaval in her life, even if she was certain she'd made the right choice.

So instead of commenting on what he'd observed, he turned his attention back to Brooke, asking her how her booth at the farmer's market had gone. She perked up a little, clearly grateful for the distraction from her worry.

As they talked about her experience at the Summer Sand Festival, Travis glanced one more time at Angela and Patrick.

He thought of his mother, who was probably getting poked and prodded by doctors and nurses even now as they waited for the results of her tests. It seemed likely that she would be all right, but this whole incident was a stark reminder that every day was a gift.

If there really was something between his sister and Patrick, he hoped they wouldn't hide from their feelings for too long.

Life was too unpredictable to wait.

CHAPTER ELEVEN

With the Summer Sand Festival in full swing, the inn was relatively quiet during the day. Everyone was either out enjoying the festival, exploring the town, or resting on the beach. Usually, Lydia enjoyed these moments—especially when Grant was around, since they could pass the time talking. But today, all she could think about was Angela's mother and her family.

Phoebe had always been so sweet and nurturing to Lydia, both when she and Angela had been kids and more recently. Lydia couldn't stand the idea of the sweet older woman being hurt or seriously ill. Angela had texted her when she and Jake had gotten to the hospital, but Lydia hadn't heard much else since then.

She sighed and stared at her phone as if that would help news come faster.

"Still no word?" Grant asked when he came back from the kitchen, a glass of iced tea for both of them in each hand.

"Nope, nothing. I hope everything is okay." Lydia accepted the cold drink and murmured a *thank you*. "People faint all the time, but it can be serious, especially for older people."

"I hope everything is all right too." Grant sat down next to her.

"Waiting is the hardest part." Lydia bit her lip, absently rubbing at her chest below her necklace as if she could loosen the knot of worry there. "Just knowing *something*, even if it's bad, is still better than having no idea what's happening. At least, it was for me."

Grant's brows furrowed in a silent question, and she sighed.

"My parents died a few years ago in an accident," she told him. "They were driving in a terrible snowstorm and skidded off the road. They were supposed to call me when they arrived back home, but I knew something was wrong when they didn't. It took a while for anyone to call."

"I'm so sorry, Lydia." Grant threaded his fingers through hers and squeezed.

"Thank you." She squeezed back, offering him a small smile. "At least I know they didn't have a painful death—it was over in an instant. And they were coming home from a nice romantic getaway, so they were in good spirits too. But even though I try to look for the positives, it's still hard. I miss them the same way I miss Paul. That same kind of aching grief, like a bruise on my heart."

"The kind that doesn't go away entirely, but gets a little less painful over time?"

"Exactly." She nodded. They had both discussed the loneliness of grief at length—it was what had brought them together in the first place, breaking down some of the barriers they'd each kept up. "I still get nervous when snowstorms hit though. At least, I do if anyone I know is driving home."

"That's understandable. My folks moved out to Arizona a while back to escape the cold, so any time there's a wildfire anywhere in the region, I get nervous. They lost one house, but luckily they were okay. Their new house is in a better area."

"Wow, from the east coast to Arizona?" Lydia raised her brows. "That's like jumping from a freezer and into the flames."

"I know." He snorted, taking a sip of his drink. "My mom's not a fan of the cold at all, and my dad's from Texas originally, so it's not too bad for them. I visited them once in the middle of the summer and vowed to never set foot there again unless it was fall or winter. Even touching the metal part of your seatbelt can give you a mean burn. It's a good thing my parents are such pleasant people. I would have seriously regretted going if they weren't."

Lydia laughed, and Grant flashed the smile that she'd come to know and love so well.

"What are they like?" she asked.

"Hmm. A bit like me, I guess. They aren't the most talkative folks out there when you first meet them, but they warm up fast. They've been retired for a while, so they spend a lot of time relaxing or enjoying the nature in Arizona when it's not as hot as the surface of the sun." He rubbed the back of her hand with his thumb. "I'd like you to meet them at some point. And they've already been asking about when they can meet you."

"Really?" Lydia felt her cheeks flush with pleasure. "You've talked to them about me?"

"Of course I have. All the time. They know about the inn and how we met, so they almost feel like they know you already."

"Meeting them would be lovely."

Being with Grant made Lydia feel almost like she was a teenager again sometimes, minus the angst. The excited anticipation of getting a call from him, meeting his parents, discovering new things about each other—she'd forgotten how much she enjoyed all of that, and how much she loved having a second set of parents.

She was still close with Paul's parents, and they had come to visit around the holidays last year, wanting to spend time with Holly as well. They cared for Lydia like she was their own daughter, and she was certain they'd be happy to know that she was moving on and finding love again after the devastation of Paul's death.

"I know you'll all get along." Grant brought their joined hands up to his lips and kissed her hand. "Maybe around the holidays?"

"Yeah, maybe then." Lydia beamed.

She glanced around to see if any guests were around so she could sneak a quick kiss, but before she could, her phone buzzed on the desk.

"It's Angela," she said, dropping Grant's hand and picking up her phone. She swiped the screen to answer and brought it to her ear. "Hey, what's going on?"

"My mom's okay." Angela's voice was soft, though still a bit strained. "She's stable, and they're running some tests on her just to rule out a few things."

"Thank goodness." Lydia looked at Grant and gave him a thumbs up. "Do they have any idea what caused her to pass out?"

"No, but the doctor sounded confident that it wasn't anything super serious," Angela told her. "They're getting the results from one test in a bit. I think I see the doctor coming, so I should go. But I'll keep you posted."

"Okay. Send her our love."

"I will. Thanks again for keeping an eye on the inn while I dealt with all of this."

"Of course," Lydia said with no hesitation. "Anytime. That's what partners are for."

They hung up, and she put her phone down and sank back into the seat. Her anxiety had eased somewhat, but not completely. She hoped Angela would have even more news soon.

* * *

Doctor Chase walked back toward Angela and her family with a chart in hand, his stride purposeful.

The lightness of his expression felt like a good sign, at least to her. Patrick was still sitting next to her, entertaining Jake with goofy jokes as he had when they'd gone to the hospital for her son's broken arm, but he paused when the doctor arrived.

"Hey, there." Doctor Chase took a seat next to Mitch, whose face was still a little pale. "We have good news from this latest test. Phoebe is going to be just fine."

The family let out a collective sigh of relief, making Doctor Chase smile a little.

"The fainting was likely related to hypotension—low blood pressure. In her case, she's healthy overall, so it seems like her episode was caused by dehydration or a change in posture," he continued.

"Ah, that makes sense," Mitch murmured. "She had reached down to get a little rock out of her shoe before she collapsed, but I didn't think anything of it when she stood back up quickly. And it's pretty hot out."

"Exactly." Doctor Chase nodded. "Fortunately, hypotension is very easy to deal with. Compression socks help, as does increasing salt intake and staying hydrated. When she's discharged, we'll give you a full breakdown of her condition and what to do to prevent it from happening again."

"Thank you so much." Mitch blew out an audible breath, standing and shaking Doctor Chase's hand. "Can we see her now?"

"Sure, in a few minutes—she's getting a fresh IV of fluids. I'll come get you again when she's ready."

Doctor Chase disappeared into the hospital again and everyone finally let out the happiness they had kept in check around the doctor. Angela hugged her dad, then her siblings, and ended up hugging Patrick last. He smelled nice, but he let her go before she could figure out what the scent was. Her cheeks went a little pink—now wasn't the time to be thinking about that.

"I should get going," Patrick said, squeezing her shoulders and glancing at her family. "See you at the inn?"

"Yeah, of course." She smiled up at him. "Thank you for coming."

"No problem, seriously." He smiled back, then said goodbye to Jake and everyone else.

Soon, Doctor Chase returned and escorted them back to Phoebe's room. She was sitting up in bed in her hospital gown, looking a little pale but fine overall. Everyone swarmed around her, rushing in for hugs and kisses on the cheek. Jake was able to climb up onto the bed with her and curled up by her side the way they always did when they watched movies together.

"Oh, careful with my IV." Phoebe shifted a little on the bed, releasing Angela from a one-armed hug over Jake's body. She wrinkled her nose. "It took them a while to find a vein on me. I'd hate to have the nurse come back and poke me a bunch of times."

"Needles are scary," Jake said solemnly.

"They are, even for grown-ups." Phoebe gently stroked Jake's hair, smoothing some blonde flyaways down.

"We were so worried, Mom." Brooke squeezed Phoebe's other hand, her blue eyes shining.

"It's going to be okay." Their mother patted Brooke's arm, giving her a reassuring smile.

"You're the one who collapsed. We should be telling *you* that," Mitch said, switching places with Angela so he could kiss his wife on the forehead again.

"Don't, seriously." Phoebe chuckled, clearly a little embarrassed about the entire thing. "It was just a little tumble. I have a few scrapes, and I have to wear some tight socks. I have to eat more salty things and stay on top of my water intake. I still have a lot of life in me, so this won't slow me down."

Angela was grateful for that. She looked at Jake

next to her mother and felt a flutter of joy and relief, knowing that Phoebe would be around—hopefully for a long time to come—to see Jake grow up.

CHAPTER TWELVE

Though he was extremely grateful for his laptop and the "delete" button on its keyboard, sometimes Patrick had to go back to pen and paper to get his ideas flowing.

He looked down at his notebook and tried to piece together his notes from the day before. His handwriting wasn't the neatest, and his notes were written in a shorthand that even *he* could hardly remember. There were scratch outs, little doodles, and symbols that looked like hieroglyphics.

"What does 'lemon tree scene' even mean?" he murmured to himself, skimming his other notes for clues.

Having finished drafting his previous book, he had moved on to plotting out the next one while his editor did work on the completed book's manuscript. He had never been the type of writer to fly by the seat of his pants without any idea of what his plot or characters were going to be. Since he wrote thrillers and detective stories, he liked to make sure that the right beats happened at the right time.

But that didn't mean his outlining process would make any sort of sense to an outsider. His notebook looked like it contained the ravings of a lunatic. There were lines connecting two seemingly unrelated things, notes written in the margins, words written perpendicular to the lines, and plenty of doodles. He knew it would all come together in a neater outline eventually, but he couldn't force the issue. Forcing it only made things doubly frustrating.

"Ah, that's right." He snapped his fingers, the memory of what the "lemon tree scene" was supposed to be popping back into his head.

The lemon tree was the site of a murder, but he hadn't figured out what things the killer was going to leave behind for the police to find. The stray notes that he had made yesterday started to fall into place, and he picked up right where he had left off before. New ideas rushed through his head, and he scribbled them down, falling into his creative zone just like he had in his office at his old house.

Although he hadn't been at the Beachside Inn nearly as long as he'd lived in that house, his room at the inn had begun to feel oddly like *home* in some ways. The bed was comfortable, and he'd settled into a daily routine. The desk was in the perfect spot, with a view of both the grassy area right outside the inn and the water. He kept the windows open for fresh air, so his room always smelled like the ocean.

"Wooooosh!" A little boy's voice carried up to Patrick's window from outside.

He stood up a little so that he could see better. It was Jake, running around with his arms outstretched beside him. One forearm was noticeably paler than the other one was, but that was much better than the cast the boy had worn for several weeks.

Patrick smiled and checked the time. Now that he understood what his notes said, he could step away and let some of his new ideas marinate in his brain. He could already envision some scenes that he wanted to start writing already.

He headed downstairs just as Angela and Jake were coming inside.

"Look!" Jake blurted, running toward Patrick with his arm outstretched. "My cast is gone!"

"I see that." Patrick grinned. "It looks great. How does it feel?"

"Good!"

Jake skipped away as he answered, likely heading into the back office, and Patrick and Angela chuckled as they watched him go.

"He's been so excited about getting the cast off that I'm nervous he'll take another fall and hurt himself all over again," Angela admitted, grimacing slightly.

"That would be terrible. A third time visiting the hospital in a few short months would be no fun at all." Patrick studied her face for a few moments. She looked much more relaxed than she had the last time he'd seen her. "How's your mother, by the way?"

"She's doing really well. She's at home with my dad, and he's been pampering her nonstop in the week she's been out of the hospital." She laughed, playfully rolling her eyes. "As much as she'll *let* him pamper her. She's so used to being the caretaker for everyone else that she has no idea what to do now that she's the one being cared for."

"I get that. I'm glad to hear she's doing well."

"Thank you." She hesitated, then added, "And thanks again for coming to the hospital. It really meant a lot to me—you kept us at ease."

"It was no problem. I'm glad I could help."

"We're actually about to head out to the beach.

Jake's getting his sandbox stuff from the back. Want to come along?" Angela asked, glancing past Patrick's shoulder for Jake.

"That sound amazing. But unfortunately, I can't. I have to head out in a little bit. Jennifer is showing me some houses this afternoon."

Patrick felt just as disappointed as he sounded. The beach, especially with Angela and Jake, sounded perfect on a day like this. The sky was mostly clear with just enough clouds to give sunbathers intermittent breaks from the sun's rays, and it was warm enough out to make a dip in the water a perfect reprieve. Despite being close to the beach, he hadn't gone down to the water to relax in a long time. He even had a book he had been dying to get into, a perfect beach read.

"Oh, right." Angela blinked, almost as if the idea of him looking for houses had dawned on her for the first time.

Patrick had to admit that Jennifer's call had surprised him too. He had fallen into the routine of living at the inn, waking up and eating delicious pastries and coffee for breakfast, taking walks on the beach, seeing Angela all the time, and writing at his perfect little desk.

When he'd first checked in, he had been itching

to find a new house, but in the past couple of weeks, the idea had fallen by the wayside almost entirely. He had always been the kind of person who could never fully relax when he had to sleep anywhere but his own bed, but the inn felt completely different for some reason. It was cozy and felt like a home, even with all the people coming in and out. He wasn't in a hurry to move on anymore.

A moment later, Jake came running, a nylon bag filled with plastic sandcastle toys slung over his shoulder and bright green sunglasses on his face.

"Ready!" He beamed up at his mother, skidding to a stop.

"All right, then." Angela took Jake's hand, waving to Patrick. "Good luck on your search."

"Thanks."

Patrick watched them leave and sighed. He had just enough time to grab whatever was left from the breakfast offerings before he had to get dressed to meet with Jennifer. He couldn't decide whether he was hopeful that he'd find a home today or a little sad at the idea that he might have to leave the inn soon.

* * *

"Hey! Anyone home?" Brooke called into her parents' house as she opened the door, even though she knew they were there. "I come bearing treats."

She liked to stop by when she had a free afternoon to offload her extra treats and say hello. She was happy to have her parents a short drive away from her apartment on Marigold, especially after Phoebe's low blood pressure diagnosis. She had resisted the urge to check in every day, since she knew her mother was a little embarrassed about the whole situation, but she felt like enough time had passed.

Mitch appeared from around the corner. "Ah, you know exactly what to say to get my attention."

"Hi, Dad." Brooke laughed and hugged him. "Where's Mom?"

She couldn't keep the nervous twinge out of her voice. Ever since Phoebe's fainting incident, the entire family had been on alert despite the fact that her diagnosis hadn't been all that serious. Everyone had been calling each other and texting in their family chat a little bit more often, just to say hello or to send a silly meme. Brooke had always loved her family, but now she appreciated everything she had even more.

"She's outside." Mitch draped an arm around

Brooke's shoulders, nodding toward the back of the house. "I have her set up with those compression socks and plenty of iced tea."

"And she's actually sitting down?" Brooke craned her neck a little to look up at him, raising an eyebrow.

Phoebe was notorious for puttering around just to fill the time, whether she was taking on a small home improvement project, planting flowers in the garden, or tidying up the house. She'd been an elementary school teacher before retiring, so she'd been used to chasing kids around and being on her feet.

"Well, she *should* be." Mitch glanced over his shoulder, shaking his head ruefully. "I've caught her sneaking around when I'm not looking, even though the doctor said she should avoid getting up and down a lot."

"Sneaking around to do what?"

"Oh, who knows? Fluffing pillows or doing dishes or anything to keep her hands busy. I'm adapting, though. I bring her pitchers of tea or water instead of one cup at a time so she won't make the excuse that she needs more water, and I bought her a bunch of new yarn to get a jump start on making things for winter," he said. "And I've been cooking all her favorite foods to entice her to relax."

Brooke's heart warmed. Her father had always been caring, but seeing him watch over her mother made her appreciate him on a whole new level.

"By *cooking*, do you mean you've been grilling non-stop?" she teased. Her dad had a few food go-tos under his belt, and he cooked them constantly. The grill was his best friend in the summer.

"Well, you caught me." He grinned. "I've been making the iced tea from scratch too, which isn't a big deal, but she likes it more."

"What kind of iced tea? I brought lemon shortbread cookies."

"Peach. It has chunks of the fruit in it and everything."

"Oh, wonderful." Brooke pulled a tin out of her pink reusable shopping bag. "These should go perfectly with the tea."

They went outside, where Phoebe was flipping through a magazine and sipping her drink at the table. Aside from the pink compression socks on her feet, she looked totally normal, and as healthy as ever.

"Hi, sweetheart." Phoebe made a move to get up as she spoke, but Brooke waved her down.

"Don't get up, I'm coming to you." She stepped

forward and gave Phoebe a kiss on the cheek. "I brought shortbread cookies. Lemon."

"Perfect, thank you! I've been getting a bit hungry."

Brooke sat at the table and put the tin of shortbread in between everyone as Mitch poured her some tea. The weather was perfect for sitting outside, especially under the umbrella. It was warm without being too humid, and they were shielded from the intensity of the midday sun.

"These are delicious." Phoebe polished off a cookie in two easy bites. "Did you sell them at the festival?"

"Nope, not these exact ones. But the ones I *did* sell went fast." Brooke had left her booth behind and sped off to the hospital after Phoebe's fainting spell, but the beginning of the day had been wonderful. "The treats all seemed to be very popular. People who didn't even know me came back around for seconds, and a few people from the inn stopped by too."

Mitch smiled, taking his third cookie from the small container. "That's great, honey."

"Yeah. It was a pretty incredible experience." Brooke remembered the faces of her satisfied customers, from the youngest toddlers all the way to the elderly. "I baked extras just in case, and I was already dipping into that supply by the time I had to leave."

"I can see why. You've worked really hard at learning how to bake well, on top of the innate talent you already had." Her mother beamed at her. "I could see you doing this for a long time."

A grin stretched across Brooke's face. "You think so?"

"We know so," Mitch put in, looking just as proud as Phoebe.

Brooke bit a cookie in half, chewing slowly as she processed their words.

They had told her all of this before, of course, but now she could truly believe them since she had seen the demand with her own eyes. She could easily imagine herself at the farmer's market throughout the year, selling pumpkin-flavored everything in the fall, warming treats in the few days the market was open in the winter, and pastries filled with stone fruits in the spring.

All she had to do was keep working at it, piece by piece.

CHAPTER THIRTEEN

Although Hunter had lived in Los Angeles for many years, it still felt a bit strange to be back, especially after the last few months of east coast island living.

The only traffic he had experienced in Marigold was foot traffic, and even that was rare. It was mostly concentrated on the boardwalk, where people gathered in the evenings to watch the sunset, or outside of popular restaurants.

There was traffic everywhere in LA, and seemingly all the time. He had spent hours upon hours sitting in his car throughout his career, staring at the bumper in front of him and willing things to move, but now it felt strange. He kept checking his watch, then checking his ride share app to see how far away they were, then looking out the window.

He had flown into LA to audition for the role of William in the historical drama he was excited about, one of the few in-person auditions he'd had in the past few years. He was established enough that sometimes the roles came to him or the casting directors were fine with him sending a video of his performance, but this was different.

Even though the source material was niche, the movie was already getting some buzz. This role was different than ones he'd had in the past, much more serious, and his career had slowed down enough in the past few years to warrant an audition. But he didn't mind. After starring in one too many underperforming action films, he'd decided to be choosier about projects, which came at a cost. And he had moved across the country on top of that.

Traffic started inching forward again, and his driver tried to switch lanes, only to get honked at. The driver muttered something under his breath and made his way into the other lane, then off the highway.

"This traffic gets worse every day," the man said with a sigh.

"It seems that way. I don't miss it." Hunter looked outside at the palm tree lined road, which was nearly as busy as the freeway had been.

Hunter truly missed what LA had meant to him back when he'd first moved there—it had represented his love of acting and his dream of actually making it in the tough business. When he'd gotten his career off the ground, he'd fallen into the glitz of it all, from the expensive clothes to the award shows to the fancy cars, before realizing that all he wanted was the core of it: acting and creating something that moved people, whether it was to laughter or to tears. He wanted the simple life and his craft, and hoped that this audition would allow him to have both.

"Where are you visiting from?" The driver glanced in the rearview mirror with a look Hunter had come to know well. He knew Hunter's face but couldn't place him.

"From Massachusetts—this little island called Marigold. I used to live here for a long time, though. I'm in town for an audition," Hunter told him.

"Ah, I knew it. I knew your face from somewhere. Those action flicks, the ones with the speedboats," the driver said. After a beat, he added, "No offense for not recognizing you at first."

"None taken at all." Hunter smiled. "It's kind of nice being a little more anonymous these days."

The driver pulled up to the restaurant where

Hunter was going to meet with his agent, Mimi Callahan. Somehow they had made it on time.

"Good luck on that audition, man," the driver said, glancing over his shoulder.

"Thanks."

Hunter headed inside the building, a bustling, brightly colored Mexican restaurant that Mimi tended to favor. He spotted her almost right away from her big blonde hair. Mimi was originally from Georgia and hadn't lost her—former—southern pageant queen exterior. Hunter always wondered if she kept up her look on purpose. It made people underestimate her until she showed them just how good of an agent she was.

"Well, look at you!" Mimi stood as he approached, holding out her arms. "How are you, honey? You look so healthy."

"Not bad, even with the jet lag." Hunter chuckled as he gave Mimi a hug. "How are you?"

"Fine, fine." They both sat. "Just dealing with clients who aren't as easy to handle as you are. Life all the way over on the east coast must be treating you well."

"It is. It's a bit of a shock being back in Hollywood, actually. I forgot how bad traffic is." He opened his menu, scanning the pages. "What's good here?"

"Go with the taco sampler. You won't regret it."

Hunter always went with Mimi's food suggestions, so he ordered the tacos. He missed the food in LA, although Marigold's food was amazing. He'd tried food from a number of local restaurants at the Summer Sand Festival and had loved everything. He'd especially loved all the pastries and cookies he'd gotten from Brooke's booth, which had disappeared almost embarrassingly fast from his kitchen.

Another benefit of leaving the Hollywood bubble was that he could indulge in good food without people looking at him with a tinge of judgment in their eyes. LA sometimes felt like it was all health food, all the time in celebrity circles.

He and Mimi made small talk, nibbling on chips and catching up, until the tacos came. The taco sampler had five tacos, which was at the upper limit of what Hunter could handle on a regular day. But he had only had an overpriced yogurt parfait and coffee that morning, so he was glad for the large portions.

He usually didn't eat a huge meal before an audition, but he still had a bit of time to digest before he went in to meet with the producers and director.

He tried to push his nerves aside and enjoy the moment with Mimi.

"How are you feeling about the audition?" she asked. "It's been a little while since you've done one."

"Nervous. Surprisingly so." Hunter polished off a chicken taco. "I've been working on the audition pieces a lot, and I think I've got it down, but I won't know until I get in there."

"You're going to do great. A little bird told me that you're already one of the director's top picks," Mimi said, somehow managing to eat her tacos elegantly. "You just have to go in there and do your thing."

"I'm a top pick?"

"You are. Top three."

Hunter let out a shaky breath and wiped his fingers on his napkin. "I'm not sure if that's good to know or bad to know."

"It's a very good thing, because I know who the other two under serious consideration are, and you're a better fit for the role." His agent grinned. "And no, I'm not going to tell you who the others are."

"You're killing me, Mimi."

"No, I'm stopping you from getting into your

own head and comparing yourself to others," she said. "Comparison is the thief of joy, hon."

"I know, I know. But you're sure? Out of everyone they're considering, I'm at the top?"

Mimi shrugged, an amused twinkle in her eyes. "I said what I said. Take it or leave it."

Hunter could only sigh and smile too. This woman could drive him crazy sometimes, but he knew she had his best interests at heart.

After lunch, he went back to his hotel room to regroup and run through the audition piece one more time. He felt like he knew the scene where it counted, deep in his emotions. He paced back and forth a little, trying to settle his nerves and center himself. His mind drifted back to Brooke's confused face before she had burst out laughing at his overacted version of this scene. He couldn't help but smile, thinking about how genuine and warm her laugh was.

Then he remembered her watching intently as he'd run the scene the way it was supposed to be done. Her entire body had shifted in his direction, and her gaze had never left him.

That did the trick. Brooke was the audience for the movie, and if she had liked it, his performance couldn't have been too far off base.

He thought back to that moment and ran through the scene again, pulling from the emotions he'd felt then. That boosted his confidence just enough for him to feel ready to take on the audition. He listened to a calming playlist on the ride over to the studio and arrived feeling fresh. He took a few deep breaths and went into the small room, which was taken up by the movie's producers and directors.

He had heard of all of them before, but meeting them in person was a different story. The director, Andy Paulson, was considered a bit of a prodigy—he was the same age as Hunter at thirty-two but had already been nominated for an Oscar. The producers, Ana Mitchell and Thom Dalston, were both highly respected as well. To Hunter's relief, they greeted him with friendly smiles and handshakes. Early in his career, he had gone to auditions where no one had said a word to him when he'd walked in.

"It's so nice to finally meet you, Hunter," Andy said. "We've been looking forward to seeing your take on William."

"It's nice to meet all of you too." Hunter gently wiggled his toes a little in his shoes, an old trick that his high school drama teacher had taught him for fidgeting without being noticed.

"Shall we start?" Ana asked, holding up the script. "I'm sure you're on a tight schedule while you're here."

"Sure, let's dive into it."

Hunter took a few moments to slip back into William's headspace, and they started the scene. He rarely felt as settled into a character as he did in that moment. He felt the energy in the room shift to focus solely on his performance. He tapped into the right feelings at the right time, and by the time he finished, he felt like a weight had been lifted off his shoulders.

Ana, Andy, and Thom all nodded in approval, smiling. Even though Hunter was in his own world when he acted, he could tell they had really connected with him. He managed to stay cool and professional about it until he got all the way back to the hotel, where he pumped his fist into the air and blasted his favorite songs for much longer than he would ever admit to anyone else.

He packed up his small bag and got into yet another car to head back to the airport, calling Mimi on the way to tell her all about how well the audition had gone. His adrenaline rush crashed when he got on the plane, and he fell asleep quickly. Before he knew it, he was landing in Boston.

After what felt like an LA-esque crawl out of the

city, he arrived at the ferry to Marigold. He was fond of the ferry—the short trip, with the island creeping closer and closer, felt almost exciting. It already felt like he was coming home, more than coming back to LA after a press tour or a vacation ever had.

Hunter leaned up against the railing as they got nearer to Marigold. The beach was busy, as it had been all summer, with families and groups of friends clustered on the sand. He spotted a woman with a long, pale blonde ponytail in a blue sundress standing on the beach, her phone raised to take a picture of some seagulls. Was it Brooke?

He impatiently waited for the ferry to crawl closer, hoping she wouldn't walk away. But by the time they were near the shore, he realized that it wasn't her. Thankfully he hadn't called her name. Still, he skimmed the crowd, just in case she happened to be there.

As the ferry docked and Hunter collected his bag, a realization dawned on him.

He hadn't just been searching the beach for *any* familiar face. He had really wanted to see Brooke in particular.

CHAPTER FOURTEEN

Lydia sighed, clicking several weeks ahead in their booking calendar to see if anyone new had reserved a room. A few had, which was good, but the slight knot of worry didn't loosen in her chest.

The Summer Sand Festival had ended, but the island was still filled with tourists getting away for the summer. The warm months in Marigold were always the busiest, even though people visited all year round, so they had to keep their rooms filled while they could. They couldn't count on the same potential customer base in the fall or winter.

Things at the inn were fine, but just barely. Any big, unexpected expense or random downturn in tourism had the potential to throw them into the red. The updates they'd made to their breakfast offerings and the rooms had been well-received, but it wasn't enough to bring in more guests.

Lydia *felt* like they were doing everything they could, though it was nearly impossible to juggle it all. How could they possibly do more? She hoped that more experienced business owners on the island could help. Her aunt Millie had brought together a few women business owners for a get-together before the inn had opened, and they had really helped Lydia and Angela avoid some of the pitfalls that often plagued new ventures.

Even though the other business owners were in very different fields—Leah owned a hair salon, Nicole owned an art gallery, and Cora owned a butcher shop—their experiences trying to build a customer base and keep things running smoothly were surprisingly universal. Lydia hoped that they would be able to offer more advice today.

After making sure Brooke was settled at the front desk, Lydia and Angela headed over to Millie's house, which was already bustling with activity in the backyard. Usually, showing up at Millie's place put Lydia at ease right away—her aunt's home was always inviting, bright, and cozy—but today, she felt like the frenetic energy of the inn had followed her there.

"Sorry we're a bit late," she said, giving Millie a hug.

"No problem at all." The older woman hugged Angela next. "I see you've brought cookies from Brooke?"

"Yes! She couldn't make it this time, but she wanted to send something." Angela handed Millie the tin of cookies.

"I'm sure everyone will love them—they were talking about Brooke's baking earlier." Millie grinned as she waved them through the house.

Leah, Cora, and Nicole were sitting around the small patio table, drinking sangria and iced tea, and they all greeted Angela and Lydia warmly. They shifted their chairs around to make room.

The umbrella over the table was just big enough to keep them shaded from the midday sun, and Millie had thoughtfully put out citronella to ward off mosquitos. The flowers planted along her wooden fence were in full bloom, filling the air with a sweet smell and attracting butterflies. Lydia wished they were meeting under less stressful circumstances so she could fully enjoy the beautiful yard.

"Oh, what cookies have you gifted us with today?" Leah asked, pulling the lid off the tin.

Leah had dyed her hair platinum blonde and cut

it just below her shoulders since the last time Lydia had seen her. Her hair always looked great—with her fashionable cuts, she was a walking, talking ad for her salon. Lydia made a mental note to get her hair cut soon. With all the changes she was making in her life, maybe she was due for a different haircut too.

"These are lemon drop cookies," Angela said. "They don't really go with sangria or iced tea, but they're still good."

"We can make them go with sangria. Anything can go with sangria if you try." Cora chuckled. "Is Brooke not coming this time?"

"No, she's manning the front desk for us." Lydia took two cookies and poured herself a big glass of the fruit-filled wine drink.

"Busy tourist season, huh?" Nicole asked. "It's amazing how much it can vary. The gallery is either completely packed or empty, depending on the time of day. Ever since the festival ended, it's been unpredictable."

Lydia bit her bottom lip and glanced at the other women around the table. She nearly replied "yes" reflexively, the way she did when people asked how she was. Usually, she said "good" whether that was true or not. But she caught Angela's eye before she spoke.

Angela looked both exhausted and wound up at the same time, like her body was being propelled through the day by coffee and sugar alone. Her usually sleek blonde hair was up in a messy bun, and her eyes had bags underneath them.

Lydia knew she would see the same look on her face if she caught a glimpse of herself in the mirror.

"It's been a bit tough," she admitted. "We have guests, and most of them leave happy, but I feel like we're constantly trying to catch up on things."

Angela nodded. "No matter how many to-do lists and pre-emptive attempts to stay on top of things we make, new things pop up. And that's on top of all the back-end things like advertising and managing the finances."

Lydia was relieved to see understanding flicker across everyone's faces.

"So is it just you two and Brooke doing everything? Front desk, back office, and everything in between?" Cora asked.

"More or less. Brooke was officially only hired to bake the breakfast offerings, but she's been doing a lot of other work to help out as well. And we have assistance from my family sometimes." Angela scooted her chair a couple inches to one side to keep the sun out of her eyes.

"Oh, honey. You guys need help," Nicole said.

Cora and Leah murmured in agreement.

Lydia instantly resisted the idea in her head. The inn was like her second child, and the idea of bringing in more help gave her the same kind of panicky feeling she'd experienced before she'd sent Holly off to pre-school for the first time.

What if something happened and she wasn't there? Would anyone else care for her baby like she would?

The worry Lydia felt must have been clear in her expression, because Leah held her hand up.

"I know it sounds terrifying, but it seriously will make things so much easier," the blonde woman said. "At the beginning, I tried to do everything from running the front desk to managing stylists to doing all the financials, and I think I went a little nuts. My mom had to step in before I tore out all my hair in frustration." She laughed, dabbing away a drop of condensation from her glass. "It wouldn't have been a good look on the owner of a hair salon."

"Same here. Even though my husband Jay and I had a lot of experience in the food industry, and we knew a lot about what we were doing, we wore ourselves down to the bone—pun totally intended—in the first year that we were open," Cora added. "It was hard on our marriage, so eventually we hired Todd to help us. He's been a lifesaver, and he helped us find our other employees. Now Jay and I can be as hands-on or hands-off as we want."

Lydia mulled that over, especially what Cora had said about her marriage. She and Grant weren't married, of course, but she didn't want a rift to form in their relationship before it really got going. If Grant weren't able to stop by the inn and steal her away for lunch sometimes, she wasn't sure how often they would be able to see each other.

"But what about the cost of hiring someone?" Angela frowned. "Our budget is already pretty tight. We'd have to shift things around to make it work. And we would have to train them."

"It's an investment, yeah, and you have to let go a little, but it's truly worth the cost." Nicole adjusted her red-framed glasses. "It's like taking off your training wheels—you'll wobble, and it might feel like you're going to fly over the handle bars, but you'll find your balance."

"Plus, all the time you gain by not worrying about the front desk or the little day-to-day things can be devoted to growing your business," Leah added. "And you can get a little more sleep."

"We definitely need more sleep." Lydia laughed.

"Seriously. Between the inn and my six-year-old, I feel like I'm caring for a newborn again." Angela took a long sip of iced tea.

"Oh gosh, you guys *really* need help then." Nicole shook her head.

Lydia pulled out her notepad and started jotting down the advice that Nicole, Cora, and Leah gave them about hiring help and what to look for. She trusted their advice and knew they would happily assist or let her bounce ideas off them if she needed to.

The topic shifted on to the tourist season, the new establishments that had popped up on the other side of the island, and things in their personal lives before they wrapped up their meeting. Everyone had to go handle their respective businesses.

"So, what do you think about hiring someone?" Lydia asked on the drive back to the inn.

The more the other business owners had talked about the hiring process, the more Lydia's panic had faded, leaving her with just a little worry. It was possible to find good employees, but they had to get the right person from the start. They couldn't afford to have someone who wasn't a quick learner or enthusiastic.

"They definitely made a compelling case for it."

Angela drummed her fingers on the steering wheel. "It sounds like the right thing to do, but handing over part of the inn to a near stranger sounds scary."

"But we'll have to do it eventually, I bet." Lydia shrugged. "And they were right—we're always talking about how we want an extra hour in the day to build the business instead of chasing off birds or dealing with issues that pop up."

"And sleep. I miss sleep."

"I do too." Lydia let out a long breath. "Let's find someone. We need the help."

* * *

Angela loved Brooke's pastries, but the crumbs they left behind drove her nuts. She sighed and swept flakes of croissant into her dustpan. They had taken her younger sister forever to make, between folding the dough, cutting it, rolling it into shape, and resting it. Angela was genuinely surprised at how much effort went into them. They were a far cry from the croissants she had sometimes picked up at Starbucks back in Philadelphia.

At least everything was being eaten, so all of Brooke's work was being appreciated. She'd even had to put out more pastries because everyone had scooped up all the croissants and their regular offerings.

She dumped the crumbs into the trash can, put the dustpan away, and headed back out front just as Patrick came down the stairs.

"Hey, good morning!" She gave him a little wave.

"Morning!" Patrick smiled. "Has it been a busy one so far?"

"It's about average. The croissants were a hit, but the clean-up has been a bit tedious. Croissant crumbs are like the glitter of pastry—I'm sure I'll be finding crumbs for days." Angela rested her hands on her hips and shrugged. "How about you?"

"It's been a little busy. I've mostly been working on the outline for my next book, which is always fun." Patrick meandered over to the front desk and leaned against it. Angela did the same. "I think I've gotten the bones of it down, and I've even sketched out some key scenes."

"That's great."

"It is. But I have a call with my editor next week about the book I recently finished, so that's always a little nerve-wracking. Who knows? Maybe it's secretly terrible and I don't even know it."

"I doubt that," Angela said. "But I get the fear of showing someone your work for the first time."

"Yeah, it never goes away, even after all the books I've written." Patrick ran his hand through his chestnut brown hair. "When I first started writing, I thought I'd eventually become confident about everything I write, but it hasn't quite worked that way. I think I stress out about a different thing with each book. I was worried about my side characters in my past book, but this time around, it's my subplots that are stressing me out."

"I can definitely relate to finding new things to worry about or ways to second-guess your work. I wonder if that's something that a lot of creative people deal with."

"It wouldn't surprise me. But if you're talking about the inn, I would say that you don't have any reason to doubt yourself. My stay here has been absolutely wonderful." Patrick gave her a warm smile. "Speaking of which, I actually came down to check out."

"Oh! You found a house?" Angela's eyebrows raised as she stepped behind the desk.

"Yup. A little two bedroom place on the western side of the island. It's just big enough for me, my office, and all my books."

"Congratulations." Angela jiggled the mouse to wake up the computer.

"Thanks. It's such a relief, although I guess I won't totally feel it until I'm settled in." He rested his elbows on the desk. "I'm excited to put another milestone behind me."

"I bet. Closing on a house is so stressful."

"Yeah. I'm just trying to take things one step at a time," he said. "I need to finish moving things out of storage since I only have my bed and a few pots and pans to get me started. And then there's decorating." He smiled. "I'm completely helpless with that, so I might ask for your help if you're willing to give me a little input."

She laughed, pulling up Patrick's reservation. "I'm happy to help you anytime. What's your weakness when it comes to design?"

Patrick thought about it for a moment, his smile broadening even more. "Is it bad that I don't even know what I'm bad at because I'm terrible at all of it?"

"Not bad at all. If I wrote a book, I know it would be bad, but I wouldn't know exactly why. Not that I've ever seriously write anything, since I can barely handle telling Jake a bedtime story off the cuff." Angela waited for the computer to finish compiling his bill. "Thankfully, he's all about me reading him books now, so I don't have to flail."

The printer cranked out his bill, and she slit it over to him across the desk. He signed it and pushed it back to her.

"Okay, that's everything on your end," Angela said, tapping the ends of the receipt pages to straighten them up. "You enjoyed your stay?"

"I loved it." He took his copy of the receipt when she offered it to him. "It really made my life a lot easier in a stressful time."

"I'm glad to hear it." She smiled.

"I hope I'll see you around," he said, picking up his bags. He sounded like he meant it.

"Me too. See you."

She watched him leave, biting her bottom lip and sighing as a strange sense of disappointment filled her.

She had known this day was coming, but it felt odd to her nonetheless. Patrick had become a regular fixture at the inn, even amongst all the chaos. She could count on him to brighten her day with a joke and to make Jake laugh or keep him occupied for a little while if she needed a hand. The thought of not seeing him come down the stairs every morning for breakfast made a little hollow pit form in her gut. She would really miss him.

She blinked and got back to finishing the last few

steps of the check-out process, unsure of what was going on in her heart or in her head. She knew they had become friends, but was the idea of not seeing a friend every day supposed to feel this terrible?

Was she developing feelings for Patrick?

Angela pushed those thoughts aside and filed away his signed receipt for their records, trying not to glance at the door to see if he might come back for something he'd left behind.

CHAPTER FIFTEEN

"Why does today feel like the first day of school?" Angela asked Lydia, who was straightening up the front desk for the tenth time that morning. "I'm not even the one starting a new job."

"Maybe you feel like a teacher does on the first day." Lydia straightened a stack of post-it notes on the desk and examined it as if shifting it an inch actually mattered. "We know Kathy will be great, but then there's the whole teaching aspect of having a new hire. We'll need to bring her up to speed on everything we've spent months figuring out and learning."

Angela and Lydia had put out an ad looking for front desk help and asked everyone they knew to spread the word. After interviewing a few possible candidates, they had hired a woman named Kathy Manning. They'd both liked her and connected with her right away, even though her style made her look like the perfect fit for Nicole's art gallery and not the inn. But her warm, friendly smile and intelligence told Angela and Lydia that they had found the right fit.

Kathy's hair was dyed red, and her bangs skimmed the tops of her eyebrows. In the two times Angela and Lydia had met her, she had been wearing a cool assortment of jewelry without going overboard with it. On her second interview, she had worn a brightly printed dress that she'd gotten from a designer who'd had a booth at the Summer Sand Festival. She was an aspiring photographer and wanted the job to help her pay the bills while she got her own business off the ground.

They liked the idea of supporting another female entrepreneur, and Kathy had a great attitude. On top of that, she'd offered to take pictures of the inn and knew enough about web design to help maintain the website. Now all they had to do was train her on the particulars of their business.

Angela hoped they wouldn't have another Water Pressure Lady guest on their hands right away. That wouldn't be a good way to start.

"Hi, good morning!" Kathy said, stepping shyly into the inn. She was wearing another fun dress printed with parrots and cute wedge heels, plus an assortment of bangles on her right wrist.

"Welcome!" Angela shook her hand, making the bangles on the younger woman's wrist jingle. "We're so glad you're here."

"I'm glad to be here too." Kathy smiled, fiddling with one of her silver rings after their handshake ended. Then she stopped suddenly, lacing her fingers together. "Sorry for the fidgeting. I think I have some first day jitters."

"No worries. Let's get you a pastry and some coffee so we can talk and break the ice a little." Angela motioned for Kathy to follow her.

They grabbed an assortment of leftover pastries from breakfast and made a fresh pot of coffee before settling down. Angela topped off her coffee with the fancy almond milk that they'd all begrudgingly become fans of, and their new employee did the same.

"Here's today's assortment of pastries—we made sure to save one of each just so you could get exactly what you wanted," Angela said. "Brooke makes them all fresh every morning. She's usually here in the mornings, but she's out running a few errands at the moment."

"Wow, these all look so good." Kathy's eyes went wide as she glanced over the treats. "I'll try this blackberry muffin."

"Great choice." Lydia pushed the tray closer to her. "All of them are delicious, not to sound biased."

Kathy smiled and broke the muffin into pieces, popping a bite into her mouth. Just like most people did when they tasted Brooke's baking, she made a quiet noise of satisfaction as she chewed.

"If everything is this good, I'm going to love coming into work every morning."

They all laughed, the last bit of nervous tension falling away from both sides.

"They're always available in the kitchen. Brooke's learned to bake huge batches of everything." Angela took a danish. "That's actually one of the first things you'll be tasked with when you start in the mornings. Brooke is usually here first thing to get everything in the ovens in time, so all you have to do is set up. Breakfast starts at seven thirty."

"Okay, sounds perfect." Kathy sipped her coffee and nodded. "And this coffee is wonderful too. I usually don't gravitate toward almond milk, but this is so nice and creamy."

Lydia burst out laughing, and Angela nearly spat

out her coffee. Kathy glanced between them, a confused smile on her face.

"Sorry. It's a long story involving a guest who had very particular needs," Angela said. "This almond milk is a result of that, and we're all a little annoyed at how good it is."

"If any of us refer to someone named Water Pressure Lady, that's who we're talking about," Lydia added. "She was incredibly difficult, and I hope we don't have another guest who tests us as much as she did during your first few weeks."

"Uh oh." Kathy's big, expressive eyes gleamed with a mixture of amusement and worry. "What else do I need to know just in case there's another Water Pressure Lady?"

"We doubt there will be since she was very, very prickly, but here's the guide to manning the front desk," Angela said. "This makes it seem much scarier than it is—we just wanted to be thorough. It covers all the areas that you'll deal with daily, as well as what to do in emergencies and that kind of thing. We'll go over the most important parts first so you can get started."

Lydia and Angela had stayed up late the night before making a big cheat sheet for managing the front desk. It had turned out to be twenty-five pages, and Kathy's eyebrows rose a little when Angela put it on the table.

At the look on their new employee's face, Angela had a moment of panic.

What if they had gone overboard? The guide really did have everything they could think of, but they knew that they couldn't anticipate literally everything. What if Kathy decided that the job wasn't the right fit for her, just from the start?

But before Angela could worry too much, Kathy opened the printed guidebook and flipped to the first page. "Thorough is perfect," she said. "Better to know then to be in the dark, right?"

"Exactly." Angela let out a breath, smiling. "Let's start from the top."

The three women went through the handbook, answering questions from Kathy and sometimes stepping away to handle guests. Kathy was able to help with a booking issue someone was having and gave another guest a great recommendation for lunch. By the time they'd finished covering the basics, Angela felt confident leaving Kathy up front.

"Just text us if you have any questions or need us, okay?" Lydia said.

"Sure thing!" Kathy gave them a thumbs up.

"She learns really fast," Angela said as they retreated to the back office.

"She does. I already feel little bit less stressed." Lydia sat down at the table and pulled out her laptop. "Except for these ads."

"Oof, yes." Angela had suggested creating new ads for the inn, highlighting some of the recent changes they had made. "But it needs to be done. So let's get into it."

They huddled over the laptop, looking over their ads and social media accounts. Angela had only known the basics of both when they had first started at the inn, but now she was mostly confident in her ability to create something eye-catching.

The new set of ads highlighted the inn's quality and personal touches, which Cora had suggested. Her butcher shop was known for its quality too, and when she and her husband started focusing on that, they gained more loyal customers.

"Does this look right to you?" Angela asked, cocking her head to the side and looking at the ad they were going to post on Instagram. "Or am I overthinking it?"

"I feel like we need a third opinion, because we *both* tend to overthink things." Lydia chuckled. "But my first gut instinct says it's good."

"Okay, let's go with it then." Angela saved the ad and set it to go up in a few hours. "I hope it's worth it."

"It will be. I'm more worried about Meredith Walters' visit." Lydia sat back in her seat. "It's coming up so fast."

Angela bit her bottom lip, worry coming back into her mind as well. "It is. But on the upside, we've only gotten good reviews lately."

"True." Lydia drummed her fingers on the table. "And with Kathy's help, we can actually tackle the to-do list that we've added about a million items to and have barely made a dent in."

"I hope so." Angela pulled up the list, anxiety making her heart flutter. There was so much to do before the travel blogger arrived. She only hoped that they could pull off everything they needed to and get a great review.

* * *

It was hot outside, but that never stopped Brooke from turning her oven on. Whenever she baked in the summer, she just opened all the windows to her small apartment and wore a tank top and shorts. She had too many recipes to perfect and too many new ideas to try to let a little heat get in her way.

She checked the timer on the cookies in the oven before heading back to her tiny scrap of counter space. Even though she hardly had any room, she loved spending time in her kitchen and having her own space. She didn't have to worry about doing all the dishes right away, and she could play her music as loudly as she wanted—without disturbing her neighbors. She danced a little to her favorite baking playlist and flipped through her notebook of recipes.

She sighed and looked at the recipe she was working on, which was littered with cross-outs and additions. The recipe was for salted caramel chocolate cookies, which had sounded brilliant in her head when she started developing it. But she couldn't get the texture quite right. The cookie was either too chewy or too crispy, and the caramel wasn't gooey enough. Then there was the whole issue of the salt...

Brooke's playlist ended, leaving the kitchen quiet. As she crossed the room to put on new music, she heard an odd sound coming from the entrance to her apartment. She froze, listening harder. Travis had made sure that her deadbolt was secure, and she never left it unlocked—even though Marigold, and her apartment building in particular, were very safe. The sound wasn't very loud, and it didn't sound threatening, so her fear lessened significantly.

But the noise kept happening. Being in an apartment building, Brooke was used to the strange ambient sounds from her upstairs neighbors, who sometimes sounded like they were practicing tap dancing routines at one in the morning, but this noise wasn't like that at all. It sounded like someone was scratching at the door very, very carefully.

"What is that?" Brooke murmured to herself, tip-toeing to her front door.

She checked the peephole and didn't see anyone, so she opened the door to look down the hall. There wasn't a person there, but she spotted a tiny kitten standing in the middle of the hallway, looking completely lost. He was all black besides his little white paws and a splotch of white on his chest and on his face.

"Oh! Hello!" Brooke said, looking around again to see if anyone was there. "How'd you get here, little buddy?"

The kitten meowed, still standing like he didn't know where to go. Brooke slipped outside, approaching the kitten carefully. To her surprise, he didn't run. Instead, he walked right toward her, letting out another squeaky meow that made her grin.

"You are too cute." She squatted down and petted him gently on the top of his head. "Did you climb up a tree to get here? Are you missing your home or your momma cat?"

The kitten didn't respond, of course, but he butted his head against Brooke's ankle. She tentatively picked him up. and he didn't fight her. He was scrawny underneath his fur, though he looked mostly healthy.

Brooke glanced at the tree in the middle of her building's courtyard, which had a branch that an agile kitten could have easily jumped off of and onto the second floor landing. It was either that, or someone had just put a kitten in the hallway and disappeared.

She stood, scratching him under his chin for a few moments, trying to figure out what to do. Eventually, she took him into her apartment and looked for a place to put him where he would be safe as she dealt with her hot pans and cookies. She decided on the bathroom since it had the fewest nooks and crannies for him to get lost in. If he could climb up a tree and leap off a branch, she figured he could probably manage to get lost in her small apartment. Inside the bathroom, she set the kitten down on a soft towel, just in case.

She snapped a picture of him on her phone so she could post it around the neighborhood to see if he belonged to anyone. When she looked at the image on her cell phone's screen, she couldn't help the little "aw" sound that spilled from her lips. The little kitten was almost supernaturally adorable. She wasn't sure how old he was, but he was young enough for his paws and eyes to be a little too big for his frame. It made him look almost cartoonish, in a cute way.

The timer dinged, drawing her attention. Brooke took the cookies out of the oven and set them on a cooling rack, jotting down a few notes about how they looked fresh from the oven. Then she went back into the bathroom and gathered the cat before knocking on her neighbors' doors to ask if he belonged to anyone in the building.

She started with her next-door neighbor Jana, who had been two years ahead of her at their high school. They weren't super close friends, but they got along well, and Brooke had watered Jana's plants when she'd gone out of town earlier in the summer.

"Hey, is everything alright?" Jana asked. Brooke could hear the TV playing in the background and

Jana's boyfriend Drew laughing at whatever show he was watching.

"Yeah. I just wanted to check to see if you were missing a kitten." Brooke held up the furry little puffball. "I found him in the hallway."

"No, Drew's allergic to cats." Jana pursed her lips as she scratched the kitten on the forehead with her finger. "But what a cutie."

"Right? I don't know how he got up here unless he's a master tree climber. He looks super young," Brooke said. "Do you know of anyone in the building who has cats?"

"Try Jeff Steele in 2B. I think he has one."

"Thanks."

Brooke went to Jeff Steele next, but he wasn't missing a kitten either. He had a spare litter box and some wet cat food though, and he offered them to her, which she appreciated. All the other tenants on the second floor had dogs—which the kitten was not a fan of—or didn't have pets at all.

"Hm, how weird," Brooke muttered to herself as she stepped back inside her apartment. "No one knows where you came from, little buddy."

The kitten had cradled himself in her arms and had somehow fallen asleep, his tiny paws stretched up toward her. She gently poked his little bean-shaped toe pads, then petted his stomach, waking him up. He gave her a startled look, his bright green eyes large in his furry face.

"Sorry," she murmured, taking the small cat into her living room. She put him down on the couch, where he curled up and fell back to sleep.

Brooke paced in front of her couch a little bit. She already liked having the kitten there, and thoughts of coming home from a long day at work to a happy, purring cat made her smile. Sighing, she went into the kitchen and grabbed two cookies to taste, plus her notebook. The kitten didn't even stir when she sat down again.

"What can I call you besides 'little kitten'? As if you can tell me what your name is." She rubbed his belly again. "What about Scratch, since you chose to paw at my door instead of anyone else's? We would never have met if you hadn't scratched at my door."

The kitten stretched, starting to purr. Brooke grinned.

Yup. The name was perfect.

CHAPTER SIXTEEN

With Kathy helping at the front desk, Lydia had much more time available in the mornings. She still ate whatever pastries Brooke had made for the day once she got into the inn, even though she could have made her own breakfast with the extra time, and her commute from the innkeeper's residence was about two minutes long, so she didn't have to rush on that end. Instead of heading in early, she chose to take a longer shower this morning to ease into the day. She even had time left over to call Holly, who was still in Europe.

"Hey, Mom." Holly's voice was bright and happy. "You caught me at the right time. I'm just finishing up a late lunch."

"What's on the menu today?" Lydia asked, leaning against her kitchen counter.

"Just a sandwich, nothing fancy. I never thought I'd actually say this, but I'm getting a little tired of tapas. Sometimes I just want macaroni and cheese."

"Really? I didn't think you could ever get tired of tapas." Lydia smiled and watched her coffee maker sputter out its last bits of brew. "It's almost time for you to come home, though, so maybe it's just that."

"Yeah, maybe." Lydia heard Holly crinkle up some paper on her end. "It's weird. It felt like this summer went by so fast. I'm going to miss everyone I've met."

"It did go by fast. How are your friends doing? Are you still hanging out with the ones who went to Spain with you?"

"Yeah, pretty much." There was a pause, and Lydia could tell her daughter was probably fiddling with her cuticles the way she did when she was a little nervous. "And I've kind of been dating this guy."

"Oh?" Lydia's eyebrows rose as she filled up a mug with coffee and topped it off with cream.

That wasn't something she'd been expecting to hear, especially after Holly had gone through her first real breakup last semester. The poor girl had taken the breakup hard, although her visit to Marigold over Spring Break had helped raise her spirits. She had fallen for the guy hard and fast, and the relationship had fallen apart in the same way.

"I know, I know." Holly laughed. "It's nothing super serious. He's Spanish and his name is Nicolas. We have a mutual friend, and we hit it off right away. Turns out he's taking summer courses at the same university where I'm taking mine, so we kept hanging out. I'm definitely taking things slower this time."

"That's great!"

"Yeah, it's nice. I guess something good came out of that awful breakup earlier this year. I learned that there's no need to go flying headfirst into something. Keeping things light is just as good too." Holly sighed softly. "Besides, we have to part ways at the end of the summer, so it wouldn't make sense to get serious."

"Well, I'm glad he's in your life and that he's making you happy, at least while you're there." Lydia sat at her kitchen table and looked out onto the water, holding the phone to her ear.

"What's going on in Marigold? How's the inn?" Holly asked.

"It's pretty good. The only reason I have a

moment to call you right now is because we hired someone for the front desk. Kathy is a lifesaver. I can't believe we waited so long to get help."

"Gosh, finally. You and Angela were going to burn out fast." A few ambient noises came through the line, indicating that Holly had stepped outside. "I'm glad you have help."

"I am too." Lydia checked the time. It was getting close to eight-thirty, so she had to leave soon. Today would be a big day, and a flurry of nerves fluttered in her stomach. "We'll have this big travel blogger staying here soon. Do you remember me talking about Meredith Walters?"

"Yeah, you mentioned her when I asked for food recommendations in Germany. She's a big deal, right?"

"Yeah, she is. She should be arriving today, and I hope things go well. She could really help us out. Her reviews get so many hits, and a lot of people visit places just because she mentioned them in her blog."

"I'm sure it'll be great!" Holly said. "The inn is incredible, seriously. It's comfy and adorable. Even the nicest places I've stayed here don't hold a candle to the Beachside. Plus, there are Brooke's pastries to draw people in, and you and Angela are there to make everyone feel welcome."

Lydia grinned, feeling better. "Have you ever considered changing your minor? You could have a future in motivational speaking, if that's something people can actually study in college."

"That would be such a mess, Mom, even if it *were* a minor I could choose. My stage fright is horrible," Holly said with a laugh. "I've got to go. I have a study group for one of my classes."

"Okay, study hard. Love you."

"Love you too. Good luck!"

Lydia ended the call and took a deep breath, putting her mug in the sink. Meredith Walters was set to check in sometime in the afternoon, so all they could do now was wait for her to arrive. Lydia walked over to the inn, finding Angela and Kathy huddled in front of the computer at the front desk.

"Good morning," Lydia said. "Is everything okay so far?"

"Yes, it's all looking great!" Kathy looked up. "We saved you a lemon poppyseed scone."

"You're the best." Lydia grabbed the scone from the front desk, biting into it with a sigh. "I don't know how Brooke does it. These seem to taste better every time I eat them."

"They're addictive." Kathy poked at the crumbly remains of her breakfast. "I can't even let myself walk through the dining area when there are treats out anymore. My willpower isn't strong enough."

Lydia chuckled. The three women went about their business for the day, trying to stay busy so they wouldn't focus on the upcoming arrival of the travel blogger. As often happened at the inn, time seemed to fly by while Lydia worked, and before she knew it, the door opened and a woman stepped inside. Lydia's heart pounded when she recognized who it was—Meredith Walters.

The blogger was much shorter than Lydia had expected, barely clearing five feet tall, but she had a confident, poised demeanor that made her seem taller. Her dark brown hair was in a ponytail and Lydia recognized her outfit as a brand that Meredith recommended for comfortable, but fashionable travel clothes.

"Hi, welcome! Are you here to check in?" Angela asked, sounding incredibly put together despite her white-knuckled grip on the back of Kathy's seat. Luckily, Meredith wasn't able to see it from where she was standing.

"I am." Meredith approached the front desk and put her bag between her feet.

"Great. Kathy here will help you get checked in." Lydia pulled herself together and smiled. "I'm Lydia

Walker, by the way, and this is Angela Collins. We're the owners of the Beachside Inn."

"So nice to meet you!" Meredith shook everyone's hands. "I've been looking forward to this trip for a while."

"We're glad to have you here. Was your ferry ride nice?"

Lydia was impressed with how calm she sounded even though on the inside, she was freaking out. She wished she had gotten in a little earlier. Did she have scone crumbs on her top? She glanced down at herself. Luckily, she was clean. She couldn't check her teeth for poppyseeds, so she just had to hope things were fine.

"It was. It was lovely to get a little sea breeze before I even arrived." Meredith chuckled. "It's so wonderful being this close to the water."

They chatted about the weather and the best waterfront views as Kathy checked their new guest in. Then Kathy nodded.

"Okay, you're all set. Angela will take you to your room." She found the right set of keys and handed them to Meredith. "Have a nice stay."

"Thanks so much." The petite woman picked up her bags and looked to Angela.

"You'll be right up the stairs and down the hall to

your left," Angela said, gesturing for Meredith to go ahead of her.

Meredith started up the stairs, and Angela shot Lydia and Kathy a thumbs up before disappearing after her. Lydia finally relaxed a little, and her remaining nerves turned to excitement. Things were off to a good start with their big guest, and she was so proud of how well Kathy was doing already, manning the front desk with a friendly and professional demeanor. She was pleased with the work they'd done and the changes they'd made at the inn.

Now all they had to do was blow Meredith Walters away.

CHAPTER SEVENTEEN

Patrick stood in the office of his new house, staring at the final few boxes he needed to unpack and wishing their contents would somehow end up on his shelves without him lifting a finger. He sighed and ran a hand through his hair.

He loved seeing his bookshelf filled with his favorites and had always kept his books in a particular order. He kept the books by his literary heroes at eye-level, closest to his desk, and reference books below that, within arm's reach. The others were split up by genre and alphabetized. He hadn't had to move them in his old home except for when he dusted. The thought of putting them all up in that order again made him tired before he even began.

At least these shelves are built in, he thought, *I'd hate to have to assemble shelves and* then *fill them.*

His move had gone as smoothly as he'd hoped, and he had already unpacked the boxes of the things he needed the most. The new house was almost feeling like a home, aside from the last few boxes that he had to step around to get to his desk.

"Just do it. It won't take long once you get started," Patrick said to himself as he grabbed his box cutter, as if speaking the words aloud would give him the push he needed.

He cut the tape on one box and ripped it open the rest of the way. It was his box of classics, which he only kept because he knew he'd miss them the moment he got rid of them. He kept his classics on the shelf farthest from his desk, just because he rarely touched them. He pulled out an ancient copy of *Jane Eyre* and tossed it on the hardwood floor with a smack, then topped it with a decorative edition of *Dracula* that his cousin had given him as a gift years ago. The books inside the box seemed endless.

After several minutes of work, his laptop chimed. With that single sound, the small bit of unpacking motivation he'd built up dissipated. It was an alert about an email from his editor, Carl.

That was much more interesting than

organizing, so he sat down and opened the message, his heart racing. He grinned when he saw the enthusiastic exclamation points in the email. Carl liked the book a lot, and although he had a few suggested changes, he didn't think the book would need any extensive rewrites.

Patrick looked through all the notes in his manuscript, then glanced at the boxes and boxes of books. Nothing terrible would happen if he left them for another day.

So he gave up on the rest of the unpacking for the moment and dove into the manuscript, starting with the scenes that his editor felt should be cut. He merged a few scenes, added some notes about which new scenes he needed to write, and rewrote ones that he had been thinking about ever since he'd sent off his draft.

Before he knew it, two hours had passed, and his back and neck were stiff from hunching over his desk. His laptop stand was in one of the remaining boxes, but he wasn't sure which one. He'd have to find it soon—it always helped him avoid this sort of stiffness. He stretched his arms into the air and peeked outside. It wasn't very hot anymore, so he decided to take a walk to reward himself.

He threw on a baseball hat and headed out,

taking the somewhat unfamiliar path toward the beach. He liked meandering walks. They gave him a chance to explore his new neighborhood. He wasn't sure where he was going, but he found a street that led to the beach. It was fairly busy, as it usually was in the summer, but since it was getting later in the afternoon, many people had headed home before dinner.

Patrick scanned the beach and grinned when he spotted Angela, her bright blonde hair standing out in the crowd even underneath the hat she was wearing. She was walking in his direction with Jake, laughing at something her son had said. Patrick couldn't stop a flood of excitement from bubbling up in his chest. It had only been a few days since he had left the Beachside Inn, but he'd missed seeing her.

He took another look around to orient himself. He wasn't far from the inn—maybe he had been walking in their direction unconsciously.

After kicking off his shoes, he stepped onto the sand, crossing the beach toward Angela. She spotted him and lit up, waving.

"Hi, Patrick!" Jake said, beaming up at him when Patrick got close enough.

"Hey, buddy." He gave Jake a low-five, which

had become their go-to greeting in the time they'd spent together at the inn. "Hi, Angela."

"Hi. How are you?" she asked, adjusting her big hat on her head so he could see her eyes a little better. They were bright with genuine happiness. "Are you all moved in to your new place?"

"Pretty much. I just have those last few boxes of things I don't really use all the time." Patrick fell into step beside her, watching Jake run ahead and kick at the waves. "It's been nice having a new space. I didn't realize how easy it is to walk to the beach from where I am."

"That's great." She looked off into the distance for a moment. "We miss having you around the inn, though."

"I miss being there too."

The same flutter of happiness Patrick had felt when he looked at Angela from afar filled his chest again, and he smiled.

* * *

Tension fell from Angela's shoulders as she and Patrick walked down the beach several feet behind Jake. The day had been so stressful that Lydia had insisted she and Jake take an afternoon at the beach.

The break had been mostly relaxing, but a cloud of worries sat in the back of Angela's mind and wouldn't leave. Seeing Patrick was a welcome comfort and distraction.

She hadn't been lying when she'd said she and Jake had missed him around the inn. She hadn't realized just how much their conversations throughout the day had helped her relax and get an extra burst of energy when she'd needed it.

Angela took a quick glance up at Patrick to gauge his expression. He still had the ghost of a smile on his lips, to her relief. She was worried that she'd said too much when she'd told him she missed him, but he seemed happy to hear it.

"How have things been at the inn? Anything weird or interesting to report?" Patrick asked.

"Things are fine. Hectic, as usual," Angela said. "On the weirdness front, a little bit. There was a guest who said she was bringing her small dog, which is fine as long as you pay the pet deposit. You know what she brought instead? A ferret. I've never even seen one outside of a pet store."

Patrick burst out laughing, the sound seeming to come from deep in his belly. "A ferret?"

"Yep. On a little harness and leash and everything, walking down the stairs like a dog." She laughed. "I couldn't really do anything about it since the pet deposit clearly stated that it covered small animals, and a ferret is one."

"Why didn't she just say that she was bringing a ferret?"

"I don't even know." Angela snorted. "Especially since she walked it out like everything was totally fine. It wasn't like she was smuggling it in or out."

"Were you able to hold it together when you saw the ferret on a leash?" Patrick stepped around a cluster of rocks, bringing him closer to Angela's side in a way that felt more intimate than normal, but not unwelcome. "I wouldn't have been able to hide my shock or my laughter."

"I just remember blinking to see if I was actually seeing things right, and then smiling as if nothing was wrong. I don't think I managed to say anything about the ferret, though, so at least I didn't make it awkward by laughing at her beloved pet or something."

"That's because you're a pro already."

"I still don't feel like one." Angela sighed.

"But does anyone really feel like a pro at anything all the time, even if it's their full-time job?" Patrick asked. "It's just like being an adult. When you're a kid, you think you're going to hit a certain age and suddenly know how to do it all, but then you realize that everyone just gets better at *acting* like they know what they're doing."

"I guess that's true." Angela mulled that over for a few moments, watching Jake throw some seaweed back into the ocean. "I've only thought like that in regard to parenting. After Jake was born, I was a real mess. I felt like I was floundering all the time, and I wondered how my own parents had managed to raise *three* kids. Then my mom told me that she'd felt the same way for the longest time, but she eventually got her footing."

"Yeah. I mean, I don't know what the parenting piece is like, but the best thing I've realized in life is that you'll find your groove eventually if you keep pushing forward."

Even with Patrick's hat shading his eyes from the sun, Angela could sense the warmth in them.

"I bet that mindset helps with your writing." She glanced up at him and smiled. "Or is that why you're taking a walk right now? Are you out here trying to find your groove?"

"No, not this time. This is a reward walk." He gently nudged his shoulder against hers. "I didn't know I'd get to see you, so this is better than I anticipated."

Angela tried to hide the pleasure in her eyes, dipping her head so her hat would hide her face from his view. She wasn't sure if she succeeded or not.

"Do you have the afternoon off?" Patrick asked after a comfortable pause.

"Sort of. Lydia had to make me and Jake come out here for the afternoon because I was close to tearing my hair out over a spreadsheet, and that's even *with* Kathy taking some pressure off of us by manning the front desk." Angela took off her hat so it wouldn't get carried away in the sudden breeze. "We're doing our best and learning as much as we can, but we can't anticipate everything. Add in all the regular ups and downs of running a business, and it's easy to feel swamped. I know I can't rush it, but I wish I had my footing already."

Patrick didn't speak, but Angela knew that he was listening to her and digesting her words. She appreciated how well he listened. He didn't just nod along, trying to look like he was paying attention. He actually focused on her, every single time, like their conversation was the only thing that mattered. Even in their passing conversations at the inn, he'd had the same focus on her words as he did now.

"If you didn't tell me all of this, I don't think I

would have guessed. You do a great job at keeping calm," he finally said.

"Honestly, I think I did a better job when you were around. It was nice to break up the day with a little conversation and laughter."

Their hands brushed against each other, almost like they were seeking out the touch. Electricity shot up Angela's arm and to her cheeks, which flushed warmly. She wasn't sure why she'd let that happen, but it felt like it was meant to. Something in the air shifted around them, like the world was shrinking to just their little part of the beach.

Patrick stopped walking, and Angela followed suit. Had he felt the same shift in energy too?

He looked at her, a mixture of wonder and apprehension on his face. Even behind his unsure expression, Angela could feel another change between them. She could tentatively put words to it —attraction? Chemistry? A new possibility? Still, she wasn't sure if she was alone in the feeling.

"Hey," he said, his voice low. "I'm not sure if I'm making this up or if I'm crazy, but are you feeling this too?"

Relief washed through Angela. He didn't have to say what "this" was—she understood what she meant. He felt the same spark she did.

"I am. I'm glad it's not just me."

She fiddled with her hat, feeling like she used to all those years ago when Patrick would say hi to her in the hallway in high school, but better. Her stomach fluttered, and she felt like she could have easily walked on air if she tried.

Patrick's eyes lit up for a moment before apprehension came back into his expression. "It's a little soon for both of us, though, isn't it? We're both barely single again."

"Yeah, it does feel a bit fast." Angela laughed and started walking slowly again to keep up with Jake. "I wasn't expecting this to happen."

"Neither was I." Patrick's fingers brushed against hers once more, but neither of them made a move to hold hands. "Maybe we should be friends for a while and see what happens?"

"I think that would be a good idea." Angela beamed. "Whatever happens will happen. But I'd definitely like to spend more time with you."

Patrick's smile returned, brighter than ever. "Me too."

CHAPTER EIGHTEEN

"All right, little Scratch is good to go." Doctor North, one of Marigold's most beloved veterinarians, rubbed the kitten's furry head as he spoke. "He's a bit underweight, but the wet cat food should help him catch up for his age. Aside from that, he's very healthy."

"Great!" Brooke smiled, running her hand down Scratch's back. "Thank you so much."

No one had claimed Scratch in the several days since he'd appeared outside Brooke's door, so she had decided to keep him. She knew she would have missed him desperately even after their short time together if his owner did show up.

Having a kitten was a big adjustment, especially since she had never had a cat before. He was already a part of her everyday life, waking her up by curling up against her neck and helping her fall asleep with his soft purring. Sure, he liked to push things off tables on a whim sometimes, and he would sometimes use her hair as a toy if she left it down, but those were small things in comparison to the affection he gave her on a daily basis.

Brooke tucked Scratch back into his carrier, and he meowed in protest.

"I know, buddy. It's going to be okay," Brooke cooed. She tucked the soft washcloth that he had inexplicably gotten attached to in the time he had been in her home back into his carrier, and he snuggled up to it.

They headed out of the vet's office, and Brooke rolled her windows down and turned up her music on her drive back home. The sun was shining brightly, and she was in good spirits. Knowing that Scratch had a clean bill of health was a massive relief. He'd had no outward signs of illness or injury, but it was always hard to know with strays. She glanced at him in his carrier in the back seat when she came to a stop at a light and smiled.

"I think I should break out that new feather teaser again when we get home," she said in the same baby voice she had used with Jake when he was an infant. "Would you like that?"

Scratch meowed in response, as if he understood, making Brooke laugh. He was very vocal, so she'd quickly gotten used to talking to him. Once again, she was glad she lived by herself. A roommate would probably think she was nuts for asking a kitten about macarons or complaining about laundry, as if the cat could do anything about it.

She pulled off again and made a turn onto the scenic route where she had run into Hunter running lines a few weeks ago. When she caught a glimpse of a tall figure strolling down the beach, she realized she'd happened upon him again.

Hunter didn't seem like he was in distress this time. In fact, he looked incredibly relaxed, as if he was walking back home from an afternoon spent resting on the beach. Brooke tapped her horn to get his attention, making him glance up. His expression brightened when he caught sight of her, and he gestured for her to stop. She pulled onto the side of the road, cutting the engine.

"Hey!" she called, stepping out of her car. "It's nice to run into you. You look like you've been having a good day."

"I am," Hunter said with a grin as he

approached. "And it must be better than running into me while I'm waving my arms around like a crazy person. Heading home again?"

"Yup! I just took my new kitty to the vet." She opened the back seat and pulled out the kitten's carrier. "His name is Scratch."

Hunter peered into the carrier, holding up a finger for Scratch to sniff. The fluffy animal butted his head against the cage door, making Hunter chuckle.

"What a sweet little guy. How long have you had him?"

"Not too long. He literally just appeared outside my apartment somehow, scratching at my door." Brooke poked her finger into the carrier, making Scratch purr like a motorboat. "I don't know how he got there. I live on the second floor of my apartment building, so the only thing I can think of is that he climbed the tree in the courtyard to reach me. Or maybe he somehow snuck in the main entrance when one of my neighbors came into the building. But either way, he found his way to my door."

"I guess he just knew you were the right human for him," Hunter said.

"I hope so." Brooke put Scratch's carrier back into the car but left the door open so he wouldn't overheat. "How have you been? No lines to run today?"

"Nope. I got the role!" Hunter beamed, his excitement clear. "Thanks for all of your help with the audition prep. It really made a difference."

"Honestly, that was all you. My terrible acting skills probably didn't do anything. You could have had a text-to-speech bot do what I did." Brooke laughed. "But congrats! That's huge news."

"Thanks! I'm really excited." He squinted a little against the bright sunlight reflecting off the water. "They've been adding people to the cast almost every day, it feels like, and there are so many actors who I've wanted to work with for years. I can hardly believe it."

He smiled at Brooke as he finished speaking. He had a gorgeous, perfect smile. His teeth were so nice that he had done a series of toothpaste commercials a while back—she still remembered the cheerful music that had played during the ads and how much the sound of it had driven her nuts.

But this smile seemed different to Brooke. It filled his eyes with a boyish excitement that was contagious. While he still had a certain movie star energy, Brooke felt like she got a peek behind the mask, revealing the regular guy who was just happy about getting a job he'd really wanted.

"When does filming start?" she asked.

"Pretty soon. I don't have an exact date yet, but I know I'll be gone for a few months." He ran a hand over his stubble-covered jaw, suddenly looking a little apprehensive. "Actually, could I ask you a favor?"

"Of course."

"Would you be able to house sit for me?" he asked. "I can pay you, and it shouldn't be a lot of work. I have a cleaning service come in once a week since there's a lot of house to tidy, and I have some plants. I'd rather not leave the house empty the whole time I'm gone."

Brooke blinked, genuinely surprised. The one time she had been to Hunter's house, she had hardly been able to stop herself from gawking. It was gorgeously renovated, spacious, and had an amazing view of the beach.

"Wow, yeah, I'm happy to help. But if you're going to be gone for several months, I'm sure you could find some short-term renters or something. It's still the tail end of the summer season, and people are probably looking for places to stay, especially if they have a big group. You could actually make money instead of just paying me."

"Eh." He shrugged. "I'd rather not worry about finding a renter."

"Okay, then I'm in!" She gently tapped Scratch's carrier. "But I'll have a plus one."

"No problem." Hunter laughed. "There's more than enough room for both of you."

* * *

Lydia had gotten used to Meredith Walters coming in and out of the inn throughout her stay, but seeing her come downstairs with her suitcases filled her chest with anxious flutters. The travel blogger's stay seemed like it had gone by quickly and smoothly. The most she had asked for was an extra towel, since she'd dropped one of hers in the bathtub by mistake.

But still, just because she hadn't asked for anything didn't mean that she loved the inn. They'd have to wait until the review was published to find out her thoughts.

"Checking out?" Lydia asked as Meredith approached.

"Yes, I am." Meredith set her bags down by her

feet with a wry smile. "Going back to real life is always a little bit of a letdown."

"It is, isn't it?" Lydia chuckled as she started the check-out process. "But at least you get to go back feeling refreshed."

"True." Meredith rested her forearms on the front desk. "Well, *if* you take time to actually relax. I've gone on some trips where I've packed every single day with activities and felt like I'd been swept away by a hurricane by the end of it."

"Same here." Lydia shook her head, grimacing a little. "Especially when I was in my early twenties. But I fell out of the habit, thankfully. Others seemed to do the same thing. I was a travel agent for a long time, and I could tell who was going to have that 'did I even breathe?' feeling by the end of it when we were planning."

"Ah, so you're very familiar with that effect, then," Meredith said. "And what it takes to run a great inn, I'm guessing."

Lydia's cheeks flushed. Was the woman suggesting that their inn was great? She pulled herself together, maintaining a professional demeanor. "Yeah, I got to hear the good, bad, and ugly of it all. I actually used to send people to your blog if they were on the fence about going somewhere."

"Really?" Meredith smiled, looking genuinely touched even though she had thousands of readers all over the world who probably told her that all the time. "That's so lovely."

"Your reviews are great." Lydia printed out Meredith's final receipt, looking over her shoulder as she continued their conversation. "It always feels like I'm there when I'm reading them. And I love how you get into the details of what makes each place special."

"Thank you so much." The diminutive woman found a pen and accepted the receipt from Lydia. "I read a bit about the history of this place before I came. The updates to the original building are gorgeous."

"Thanks! Angela designed everything. She was an interior decorator back in Philadelphia before she moved back here after about ten years away," Lydia said. "I used to stay here every summer growing up, so I knew the vibe the older version had. That's how we met and became friends—over summers spent together in Marigold. We hadn't seen each other in years before we both ended up in town again not long ago. The inn was on the market, and the minute we saw it, we knew we had to go for it."

"Wow, you two did all of this yourselves?" Meredith asked, seeming impressed.

"With the help of our families, friends, and a few contractors." Lydia chuckled. "But we did a lot of the updates ourselves. It just felt right. I loved this place like another home growing up, and I wouldn't have had it any other way. Everything seemed to click into place at the right time for both of us, and working on it gave us a fresh start. A second chance."

"I love that." Meredith nodded and smiled in understanding as she signed the receipt. "Thank you for everything. I've got to catch the ferry. Best of luck in the future."

"Thanks, Meredith. And thank you so much for giving our inn a try."

Lydia held her breath until the travel blogger was out the door, then exhaled. It was over. She hoped that Meredith's kind words during their conversation boded well, but no matter what happened, Lydia was proud of their little inn.

CHAPTER NINETEEN

Even though they had been having family dinners almost every week for months, Angela always underestimated just how much energy her parents' house could hold at once. Between Mitch playing a loop of oldies that made Brooke groan in jest, Jake running around with Travis inside, and Phoebe puttering around the kitchen finishing up the food, Angela was almost overwhelmed.

But she loved it, and so did Jake. She and her family had always been close, but being able to do this every week was a gift that Angela didn't want to give up any time soon.

"Food's ready!" she called, bringing a big bowl of salad to the dining room table.

Everyone made their way into the large dining

room and settled down. Mitch and Phoebe had purchased a bigger table just for occasions like this, so now everyone had a little more breathing room. Everyone plated up their food, which they'd voted on in their family group text. They hadn't been able to decide between Italian or fish, so Brooke had come up with the idea of polenta that everyone could customize with whatever toppings they wanted.

Angela served herself a heaping bowl topped with grilled sausage and helped Jake top his with chicken and extra cheese. Travis had brought Ladera Sauvignon Blanc that went perfectly with it all, and all the adults got a glass of the fruity white wine. The entire meal was always great, but the first few bites were the best—the creamy polenta melted in Angela's mouth, just salty enough without being overpowering. It was the perfect meal after a long day.

"Guess what?" Brooke asked once everyone had gotten their initial fill. "I get to house sit for Hunter Reed."

"What? How?" Angela asked. "I'm so jealous!"

She had dreamed about his beautifully designed house for weeks after she, Brooke, and Lydia had gone over to discuss Hunter's now-abandoned plans to build a hotel on the piece of land he'd bought on

Marigold. He had pieces from all of her favorite furniture brands and art from artists that she had only seen online and pined over. It was a house fit for a movie star for sure.

"Well, I ran into him a while ago when I was driving on that back road that butts up to his property. He was rehearsing lines and getting super into it, so much so that I thought someone was drowning." Brooke shook her head, her cheeks turning a little pink. "I stopped my car and ran at him like a maniac trying to help. He looked totally shocked and confused until he realized that I couldn't hear him talking about a duel and not yelling for help."

Everyone laughed, and Angels joined in as she reached for the polenta to serve herself another small scoop.

"He must have been doing a convincing job," Travis said.

"He was. That's what he'll be away filming," Brooke told them all. "So Scratch and I will have plenty of room. I hope I don't lose him in there."

"Can I play with Scratch there?" Jake asked, excitement gleaming in his eyes.

As Angela had expected, Jake was completely in love with Scratch and had been since Brooke had texted a picture of him to everyone. When Brooke had watched Jake one afternoon, his love for the kitten had been cemented. Now all he could talk about was cats and kittens. Angela hoped that he could get a big enough fill of Scratch so he wouldn't start asking for a cat of his own.

"Of course." Brooke smiled over her glass of wine, then shifted the topic. "What is everyone else up to? Anything exciting? What about you, Travis?"

"Why me in particular?" Travis asked with a snort, an eyebrow going up.

"Because you seem to be at work or at the gym every time I ask," Brooke shot back, giving him the kind of grin only an older sister could manage.

Travis swallowed a bite of polenta and shrugged. "Well, that's still the case. It's been busy with all the tourists here for the summer, but it's all good. And I do go out sometimes. I can be fun, believe it or not."

"When was the last time you went out for the night? Or on a date?" Angela asked. Travis opened his mouth to answer, but before he could, she added, "And hanging out with the same two guys from work doesn't count as shaking up your routine."

Angela and Brooke shot each other mischievous looks over the table. Travis was a friendly, easy-going guy, but he mostly stuck with a few close friends instead of a big crowd. But in the time Angela had been living on Marigold again, she hadn't heard him talk about them much at all, and she knew he hadn't had a girlfriend in a while either. She hoped he wasn't getting overworked or letting himself become too isolated.

Travis sighed in resignation, making Angela grin wickedly. When she and Brooke teamed up, they could get any information out of him, and he clearly knew it. "Okay, I admit it's been a while. I've been thinking of getting back out there more."

"Like dating?" Phoebe asked, leaning forward a little as she picked up her wine glass.

"Yeah, I guess." Travis sat back in his seat. "I just don't know where to meet someone. I'm not really into the dating apps or anything like that. I met my past girlfriends through other friends, but it's starting to seem like everyone my age is settled down or taken."

"Oh, I'll help!" Brooke perked up, pulling out her phone from her back pocket. "Want me to help you set up a profile somewhere?"

"Wow, Brooke, relax." Travis smiled a little but waved her off. "I didn't say I needed a date *right away.*"

"Okay, after dinner then. We can set up your

profile while we eat dessert. I made blackberry pie." Brooke put her phone back, grinning widely. "And I brought ice cream too."

"At least the pie will soften the misery of swiping, I guess." Travis shook his head as he topped off his wine.

"You'll be fine. You're a nice guy, and you have a good career. That alone makes you way more appealing than a lot of the options out there."

Brooke sighed in resignation as she spoke, and Angela glanced her way. Angela knew that her younger sister had tried a few dating apps in the past but hadn't had much luck. With everything going on at the inn, Brooke had been totally focused on helping out and keeping up with all the baking recently anyway.

"All of these apps these days." Mitch chuckled ruefully. "It sounds like it could be a blessing or a curse. You could end up meeting someone you might never have met otherwise, sure, but it feels like there's a lot to it. Then again, I'm old, so maybe I'm not meant to understand the ins and outs of internet dating."

The oven beeped in the kitchen, signaling that it had finally finished preheating. Brooke got up to warm the pie so it would be ready in time for dessert.

Angela couldn't wait to top the scrumptious pie with vanilla ice cream and dig in. Brooke had tested out the recipe for the pie a few weeks ago, and Angela hadn't stopped asking for her to make it again since.

"Some of my friends have met their boyfriends or husbands online." Brooke shrugged as she made her way into the kitchen. "But before they did, I got an earful about their experiences with the dating sites and apps. Then again, I get an earful of the Marigold dating scene from them no matter where they meet people."

"It sounds hard no matter what you end up doing." Phoebe squeezed Mitch's upper arm and looked at him with affection. "We lucked out, didn't we?"

"We sure did." Mitch looked back at his wife as if she were still his young bride. "If I had actually skipped out on that party, who knows where we would be?"

"I know. And to think you wanted to miss the party to take a nap!" Phoebe said with a laugh.

"Well, I *was* really tired. Those were the first words you said to me—'why do you look so tired?'"

Angela was about to chime in to gently tease her parents about the story she had heard a thousand times in her life when she felt her phone buzz in her pocket. She pulled it out just in case it was an issue at the inn. She couldn't help but smile when she saw that it was Patrick texting her. She had no idea why he was sending her a message, but she was happy that he had.

Brooke must have noticed the name that flashed on Angela's cell phone as she went back to her seat, because she raised her eyebrow at Angela, a tinge of a smile on her lips.

Angela's cheeks flushed. Was her crush that obvious?

She and Patrick had agreed to just be friends, even though they both knew there was something more there, but that didn't stop her from feeling a bit giddy when he texted.

No one else seemed to notice her goofy smile, thankfully. Otherwise things might have shifted to the awkward conversations they'd had around the table when Angela had been in high school and a boy had called during dinner.

Angela surreptitiously checked the text, then gasped. Patrick's message read: *The review from Meredith Walters is up!* He had included a link at the end of the message, and she pressed it quickly. She hadn't expected the review to be posted so soon. It felt like Meredith had just left. She had figured that they had at least another two weeks to mentally prepare for it.

"What's wrong?" Travis asked, his blue-green eyes widening as he noticed her reaction to the message.

"The review is in. From that big blogger." Angela's fingers trembled as she gripped her phone, and she watched the screen until the link loaded.

The title simply said, "Marigold Island's Beachside Inn" with a photo of the inn below. Angela didn't recognize it as one they had taken. She held her breath as she scrolled down to the rating at the top. Then a massive smile spread across her face.

"Yes! She gave us five stars!"

Everyone cheered, their faces lighting up with excitement. But even though the star rating was great, Angela's fingers were still trembling. Her anxiety had quickly flipped into an abundance of excitement. What had Meredith liked?

"Read it to us." Brooke leaned closer, perching on the edge of her seat.

"'In my decades of traveling and blogging, I've seen small town hospitality change. The charm moves out with every new chain hotel or restaurant or bar that moves in," Angela read, her heart beating hard in her chest. "But some destinations have managed to provide the excellent service and accommodations that one would expect from bigger operations and seem like they're an organic thread in the fabric of their city or town, or in this case, island. Marigold Island's Beachside Inn accomplishes just that and encompasses everything you'd look for in a charming New England getaway."

She paused to clear her throat, feeling a lump form before she pulled herself together again. She could hardly believe what she was reading, but she knew she wasn't dreaming. She could taste the spice of her sausage polenta on her tongue and felt warmth from the pre-heated oven seeping into the dining room, so she was definitely awake. This was really happening.

"'The moment you walk through the door, you're greeted by the friendly faces of people who truly care about you and treat you like a friend,'" Angela continued. "'And everything else is treated with the care you would extend to your family, from the uniquely designed rooms to the absolutely incredible pastries, which are baked in-house every day. I wish I had grabbed a few for the road.'"

Brooke squealed with delight, looking a little misty-eyed just like Angela was. Angela squeezed her sister's hand.

She kept reading the review aloud, her heart warming more and more as she did. Meredith covered the history of the inn and its revival, praising Angela's design work, and talked about the wonderful conversations she'd had with other guests over breakfast. She noted things that Angela never thought the guests would think that much about, like the doors they'd installed which were designed to close quietly and the local soaps and shampoos they had stocked in every bathroom. Meredith appeared to have loved every last detail.

Meredith's experience had been everything that Angela and Lydia had hoped for—she had felt welcomed and relaxed, and she'd gotten to know people she might not have met otherwise, just like Angela and Lydia had as young girls. And she'd loved the rest of Marigold too, mentioning several of the businesses that Angela had come to adore as well.

"'If you're looking for a getaway where you'll actually get away, you can't go wrong with the Beachside Inn,'" Angela finished, putting her phone down on the table. She bit her lip, blinking away a few happy, overwhelmed tears. "Wow. This is even better than I dreamed."

"Congrats, sweetheart," Phoebe said. "You two

deserve it. You've worked so hard to make this happen. And Brooke too! It's so exciting that her pastries were mentioned."

"We're so proud of you. I think this moment deserves a toast," Mitch declared, raising his glass. "To the inn."

Everyone echoed him and clinked their glasses together. Angela was glad that she had gotten the news when she was with her family. They were a big part of the inn's success too, from helping her and Lydia update the place to giving her a hand with Jake whenever she was overwhelmed and stressed. She couldn't have done it without them.

A moment later, Angela's phone started ringing. She glanced down at the screen and then back up at her family. "It's Lydia. Let me grab this quickly."

She stepped away from the table so that she wouldn't interrupt the others with her call, leaving them to continue chatting and eating as she headed into the other room. After swiping to answer, she lifted the phone to her ear.

"Did you see it?" Lydia asked the moment Angela answered.

"Yeah. Patrick sent it to me."

"I can't believe this is happening." Lydia's voice

sounded a little thick with emotion. "I can't believe I'm actually crying."

"Don't be embarrassed. I got really misty-eyed too."

Lydia chuckled, the sounds still a little watery. "I'm glad I'm not alone. I'm just so proud of everything we've done. We really did it."

Angela grinned, blinking a few times to clear the tears from her eyes. "We did."

CHAPTER TWENTY

"Just one more second," Lydia said to Grant, darting into the office to double-check that her last email had actually sent. "I promise!"

Leaning over the desk, she quickly skimmed the inn's email inbox. It was blowing up with questions and had been for the past few weeks. Between Meredith's incredible review, their big marketing push, and Kathy's help, the inn was still doing well despite the end of the summer coming around. They had more and more bookings, with a good amount of rooms reserved even into the fall and wintertime.

Lydia was thrilled, but the bigger workload on the business side left her feeling a little overwhelmed some days. It was good, though. She preferred to be happy and busy rather than anxious and busy.

Grant chuckled. "All of these single seconds add up to minutes, you know."

"I know, I know." Lydia had to smile at that as she put her computer to sleep and straightened. "We still have time before the ferry arrives. Let's go."

They walked out to Grant's car, hand in hand, and kept holding hands as they drove to the ferry to pick up Holly, who was visiting for a little while before school started up again for the fall semester at the end of September. Lydia couldn't wait for the two of them to meet, and she knew her daughter was looking forward to it too.

Since Lydia and Grant had made their relationship official, they had fallen into an easy rhythm with each other. Grant would stop by for lunch when he could, or they would take an afternoon walk on the beach if Lydia could get away. They'd been to several of the most recommended restaurants on Marigold and had a list of several more to try out. Nearly all of Lydia's free time was spent with him, but she didn't mind in the slightest. Every day she was with Grant was a good one.

They arrived at the ferry dock just as the ferry finished pulling in. Lydia checked her texts just to confirm that Holly had actually made it onto the boat.

"Okay, she's on this one," she said, her eyebrows going up as she finished reading the text. "And she's not alone."

Holly had hinted that she would have a guest, which was totally fine with Lydia. There was enough room for everyone. But she had been expecting one of Holly's friends to tag along—another girl from school, maybe.

"Who is she with?" Grant asked, looking askance at Lydia's stunned expression.

"The boy she met over in Europe, Nicolas." She tucked her phone back into her purse, trying to shake off her surprise. "I thought it was just a short-term thing while she was overseas, but I'm guessing they didn't want to break it off yet."

They waited until Holly stepped off the ferry, holding Nicolas's hand. The boy was tall and lanky, with short brown hair and a shy look in his eyes that was clear even from a distance. He was loaded down with both of their bags. Holly had dyed a streak in the front of her dark hair blonde and looked like she had gotten a lot of sun.

"Hey, Mom!" Holly called, waving. She threw her arms around Lydia and gave her a squeeze. "I missed you so much."

"I missed you too, honey." Lydia ran her hand up

and down her daughter's back. "It's so good to see you. And I'm happy to finally be able to introduce you to Grant."

Holly gave the gruff older man a hug too, and although his eyebrows jumped a little in surprise, he hugged her back. Lydia couldn't help but smile. She'd talked about him often on her phone calls with Holly, but finally seeing the two of them face to face warmed her heart.

"It's nice to finally meet you. I've heard so much about you." Holly stepped back and squeezed Nicolas's arm. "And this is my boyfriend, Nicolas."

"Nice to meet you both," Nicolas said quietly, shaking their hands. He had a hint of a Spanish accent, though Lydia knew he had spent some time in America growing up. Holly had told her that his father was American, so Nicolas had dual citizenship.

"It's so good to finally see you in person!" Lydia said, patting his hand gently before releasing it.

She hoped she was putting him at ease. He looked like he was going to faint at any moment. She understood the anxiety around meeting the parents of the person you were dating for the first time, especially at that age. Every move felt like it had massive consequences.

"Should we head out?" Grant suggested, taking one of Holly's bags away from Nicolas. "I'm sure you're both hungry."

Holly nodded with a grin. "Definitely."

They walked to the car and drove back to the inn to drop off their stuff. Grant went into the inn to say hello to Angela while Lydia got Nicolas and Holly settled in the innkeeper's residence. When Nicolas stepped into the bathroom to freshen up before they left, Lydia took the chance to shoot Holly a pleased but surprised look.

"He's quiet, but he seems very nice," she said softly. "I didn't know you two were still dating."

"I know. I'm surprised too." Holly glanced down the hall in the direction of the bathroom. "We both thought it would just be a summer romance, but we didn't know how hard it would be to break it off. We didn't feel ready to let it end, so we're going to try long-distance. He's transferring to a school in Boston to finish up his undergrad degree, so it shouldn't be super hard."

Lydia nodded, trying to hide her wariness. Relationships in college were already difficult, but adding in distance made it even harder. "That's not too far away, especially if you pass through there to get here."

"Yeah. It's way better than me being up in Syracuse and him being all the way in Spain." Holly adjusted her ponytail, perking up when Nicolas came out of the bathroom.

The look the young couple gave each other put Lydia a little more at ease. Nicolas clearly adored Holly, and she adored him right back. Lydia trusted her daughter's judgment.

They met up with Grant outside the inn and debated briefly among themselves about where to go to eat. Both Holly and Nicolas wanted something that felt like New England, so they decided to go with some tasty comfort food at a little restaurant in town that Lydia and Grant enjoyed.

"How does it feel to be back in the States?" Lydia asked, turning to look at Holly and Nicolas in the back seat. They were holding hands, just as they had when they'd walked from the inn to the car.

"Weird. I forgot how different everyday things are," Holly said. "Like the cars are so big, and there's just so much space."

"How long has it been since you've visited, Nicolas? Holly said your dad is American." Lydia smiled, hoping the young man would relax a little.

"It's been about four years," he said in his lightly accented voice. "I also forgot how spaced out everything is and how wide the highways are. Everything is bigger here."

"And we aren't even in Texas," Lydia joked.

That seemed to do the trick. Nicolas grinned, some of his nervousness finally appearing to ebb away. "True. I think that would be an even bigger culture shock."

Holly smiled widely and launched into a story about her first time in a Spanish grocery store. The four of them chatted easily for the rest of the drive into town.

Once they arrived at the restaurant, the host settled them at a table in the corner that gave them a good view of the water off in the distance. The dishes were family style, so they decided on summer corn chowder, grilled shrimp, and a few smaller plates to share.

"So, how did you two meet?" Grant asked Nicolas while they waited for the waiter to bring their food. "Have you been dating long?"

"We met through a friend at a party," Nicolas said, looking at Holly. "We were studying at the same university in Spain, so we started to bump into each other on campus, and eventually I worked up the courage to ask her out."

"I see. And what are you studying?"

Grant studied Nicolas as he spoke, clearly sizing him up. Lydia had to duck her head and hide her smile behind her hand. By now, she knew that Grant's gruff exterior was mostly a front, but Nicolas didn't.

"Biology." The dark-haired young man took a big gulp of his water, his Adam's apple bobbing up and down. "I want to go to medical school eventually, but I also want to see if I like research."

"Mm." Grant laced his fingers together and nodded. "Very good."

Lydia bit the inside of her cheek to stop herself from laughing. Grant was in full-on fatherly mode. She half expected him to ask what Nicolas's intentions with Holly were and whether he would vow to protect her with his life.

"Are you going to ask him about his five-year plan next?" Holly teased, rolling her eyes and grinning over her glass of iced tea.

"Well, do you have one?" Grant asked Nicolas, finally breaking into a smile to let the young man know it was all in good fun.

They all laughed, the atmosphere lightening right away. As it turned out, Nicolas *did* have a very loose five year plan, which he told everyone.

Eventually the food arrived, steaming hot. Lydia's mouth watered at the sight of it.

Nicolas had never had any kind of chowder before, so they all watched in amusement as he took his first few bites. He gave it a thumbs up and quickly downed the rest of his bowl. Lydia and Grant had ordered the soup before, but it was just as delicious as she remembered—creamy, but not too heavy or too sweet. The shrimp was perfectly grilled and was a nice accompaniment to the chowder.

Soon, the topic shifted from New England's cuisine to Spain and the Spanish language. Lydia's heart swelled as she watched Grant listening to Nicolas and Holly's stories, asking genuine questions and hanging on their every word. She loved how much Grant cared about Holly's well-being, along with her own. Even though Holly was out of the nest and living on her own now, Lydia was glad that he could act as a father figure.

As the meal wrapped up, Holly leaned over to whisper in Lydia's ear as Grant and Nicolas laughed together.

"I totally approve of your new beau "I really like him."

Lydia beamed. "I'm so glad you do."

"And I'm glad to see you so happy." Holly

squeezed Lydia's hand, and Lydia squeezed hers back.

It was so wonderful to have her daughter back home, even for just a little while.

* * *

Angela had fallen in love with The Vintage Collector when she'd first moved to Marigold. Their antiques were high quality yet reasonably priced, and the people who worked there were always incredibly helpful. Plus, they even had an area with toys for kids to play with so they wouldn't end up knocking over anything expensive.

She had been there enough times that Jake ran over to the play area without being asked to, leaving her to meander the aisles of the store. Antique shopping was one of her favorite things to do, especially when it was for the inn. She was surprised at how much decor she could switch up, just to keep things fresh.

Angela paused at a display of anchor sculptures made of wood and picked one up. It was a perfect fit for one of the smaller rooms that had nautical pieces throughout. She took a quick picture and sent it to Lydia with the message, *Yes/no?* before moving on.

There were a lot of new finds, especially toward the back. One vintage doll caught her eye, and she snorted so loudly that she covered her mouth to stifle her laughter.

It was definitely an antique, because Angela couldn't think of a single child today who would have willingly played with such a toy. Its features looked both old and young at the same time, like a baby in a medieval painting, and whoever had painted on the expression had made the doll look like it was grimacing. The dress it had on was well-made, but it was in a sickly green color that somehow made the doll look worse.

"Who are you even for, you weird little thing?" Angela muttered to herself, snapping a picture.

She knew that Patrick would get a kick out of it, so she sent him the picture along with several question marks. He responded moments later with a horrified emoji and the words, *I don't know whether to laugh or cry or both.*

Angela let herself laugh without holding back. She had been texting Patrick like this ever since he had sent her Meredith's review, and his texts had become a highlight of her day. They were definitely still just friends, as they'd both agreed to be, but every conversation they had brightened her mood, whether it was via text or on the phone.

She moved past the strange doll onto a collection of old paintings, once again giggling at one. It was an oil painting of a very irate-looking goose and a child eating an ice cream cone that was so tall that it went above his head. Was the goose angry at the child? Who had put together the cone? What was the painting trying to say?

Not sure how to feel about this one either, she texted Patrick along with a picture. *Am I supposed to sympathize with the goose or the child? Or either of them at all?*

She stepped aside so that she wasn't blocking the aisle as she waited for Patrick's reply.

I have no idea what I'm supposed to feel, but I do know that if I were that kid, I'd run. Geese are terrifying, was his response. *And they'd probably steal his ice cream.*

Angela strolled through the aisles, looking for more weird finds. She sent Patrick pictures of odd lamps in the shapes of horses in the discount section, more angry geese in figurine form, and a portrait of a very annoyed looking teenager with a bad haircut from the early twentieth century.

Patrick shot back joke after joke, and Angela worried that the others in the shop were going to think she was nuts from laughing so much. But after thinking about it, she realized she didn't really care. Combining antique shopping with Patrick's commentary made the whole experience much more fun. It felt like he was right here with her, and it made her chest feel warm and full in a way it hadn't for a long time.

Her feelings for Patrick had gone way beyond her old high school crush, which had felt monumental at the time. All she had really known about him then was that he was the cutest guy she'd ever seen, and that he was really nice to everyone. Now she knew him a lot better, and she liked all of him, both inside and out.

It wasn't just his sense of humor that drew her to him—it was his intelligence, the way he listened and supported her with his entire focus, and the way he got along with Jake. Being with him was easy in all the ways that mattered to her. And on top of that, he was still incredibly handsome.

Angela realized that she was wandering aimlessly and that she had gotten way off task. She went back over to the anchor sculpture that she had spotted initially and took it to the front to buy it. Once she did, she gathered up Jake.

They were close to the Sweet Creamery and wanted to pick up something for after dinner, so they headed in that direction. Jake held her hand, swinging their joined hands back and forth as they walked and humming an off-key tune.

Her phone buzzed in her purse again, and she checked it. It was another text from Patrick, a yearbook picture of himself. He was probably a freshman in high school and his haircut was eerily similar to the surly teenager's in the portrait at the antique shop, although Patrick's image had a smile plastered on his face.

His text read: *Life imitating art?*

Angela snorted and texted back before tucking her phone into her purse, smiling at the private joke.

"You've been laughing a lot today, Mommy," Jake commented, glancing up at her. "You seem really happy."

Angela looked down at her son, who went back to humming like he hadn't said anything important at all.

But even if he didn't quite understand how insightful his words were, he was absolutely right.

Angela was truly happy.

CHAPTER TWENTY-ONE

Travis drummed his fingers on the armrest of his patrol car as he drove through town, letting out a quiet sigh. He loved his job, but some days felt like they dragged. His morning had been filled with paperwork and calls from some elderly residents who insisted that something suspicious was afoot in their neighborhood. Those kinds of calls came in from time to time, and although there was rarely anything sketchy going on, it was his duty to make sure everyone was safe.

He made it his goal to treat every citizen of Marigold as if they were his family. Even if they were calling about a fallen tree that looked vaguely like a person for the tenth time in two weeks or complaining about yesterday's traffic, he never brushed off their worries or outwardly expressed his annoyance.

As he drove, the quiet of his car was broken by the sound of dispatch calling through the radio.

"We have a code two on the north side of the island. Any officers in the area, please report," the dispatcher said. It was a new guy Travis hadn't gotten to know well yet, but he recognized the voice.

"I'm heading in that direction," Travis responded, making a right turn. "I've got it."

"Gotcha, sending the address through. No injuries were reported, but it's one woman alone."

"On my way."

Travis frowned a little and turned on his lights. Code twos were break-ins, which they usually got at night. It was a little past lunch, so what was going on? Summer always tended to have more crime for a variety of reasons, and this summer season was proving to be no exception, but still, a midday break-in was unusual. That was bad news.

He made it to the house in less than five minutes, spotting a blonde woman waving in his direction as he pulled up. She was dressed with polished professionalism in a soft pink dress and heels, and her hair was pulled back into a ponytail. He could see the worry on her beautiful face before he even got out of the car. Something in her eyes triggered his protective instincts—that urge to take care of others that had prompted him to join the police force in the first place. He needed to make sure she was all right.

He quickly rolled to a stop and parked before hopping out.

"Hello. I'm Officer Collins." Travis introduced himself, extending his hand. The woman shook it. "You called about a break-in? Are you okay?"

"I'm Jennifer Lowry. And yes, I did. And I'm fine." She looked over her shoulder at the house, which looked perfectly fine from this angle. Even so, Travis stepped between the house and Jennifer, just in case.

"Is it your home?"

"No. I'm a real estate agent." She gestured to the sign on the lawn, which read "Titan Real Estate Partners" in dark blue letters above her name and phone number. "I had a showing for this house set for this afternoon—I've been showing it for the past week or two—and came by to make sure it was staged and set to go. I walked through the house and saw that the back window had been totally smashed."

"Can you show me?" Travis asked.

"Of course."

She walked up the driveway and across a little

path that ran along the side of the house, her high heels clicking on the concrete. Sure enough, the back glass door had been smashed in, leaving pieces inside the house and on the porch.

"Do you know if anything was taken, or if there was anything of value inside the house?" Travis questioned her as he led them around to the driveway again.

"I don't think anything was taken. I just saw that the window had been broken and booked it out of there, just in case whoever did it was still around." She chuckled nervously. "I know it sounds silly since it's the middle of the day, and whoever the culprit is, they're probably long gone, but..."

"It's not silly at all. Better safe than sorry." Travis smiled a little. "Let me go inside and take a look. If you'd like to go stand by my car, I'll be back in a moment."

Jennifer nodded and headed down to the sidewalk while Travis went in through the front door. Everything looked fine until he got to the living room. Chests of drawers were open as if someone had been rifling through them, and some things were clearly out of place. The house was largely empty of all the knickknacks that a home would usually have, so there wasn't much to take.

Travis went back outside, glancing toward the street as two of his fellow officers pulled up. The three of them inspected the crime scene together and asked Jennifer a few more questions before his colleagues headed out to return to the station and file the official report. That just left Travis to finish up with Jennifer.

"It's all clear. It seems like someone targeted the house because it was unoccupied but didn't consider that it would be empty." He shrugged. "It doesn't seem like anything was taken."

"That's a relief." Jennifer fiddled with her necklace, which had a starfish charm on it. Her nails were painted a slightly darker shade of pink than her dress. "I'm glad the family was fully moved out. We just staged it with furniture that they weren't going to take with them."

"That is a relief." Travis nodded, studying her face to see if she was still worried. She seemed more at ease now than she had been when he'd arrived. He blinked, realizing he was staring at her. "So, we'll get the report filed and keep you updated."

"Thank you so much for getting here so fast," she said, her light brown eyes shining. She wore just enough makeup to bring out the tiny flecks of gold in her irises. "I really appreciate it."

"No problem at all." He dug into his pocket and found his card, then handed it to her. "If you see anything else suspicious at any of the other houses you've been showing, feel free to call."

"I will."

She smiled as she spoke, and to Travis's surprise, he felt his face get hot. It had been a while since he'd found a woman so pretty that a simple smile made him transport back to being an awkward teenager. He hoped she didn't notice.

He quickly said goodbye to Jennifer and hopped back into his car, taking a breath to center himself again.

As he drove back across the island toward the police station, he thought of the card he'd left with Jennifer—the one that went directly to his line. He didn't want there to be any more break-ins on the island, but he couldn't help but hope she'd find another reason to call.

* * *

Brooke sang along to the music she always put on whenever she baked, wiping down the massive quartz island in the middle of Hunter's kitchen. Baking and cooking in his huge, fancy house was an absolute dream. She had never had more space to work in her life, not even at the inn.

In the time she had been house-sitting, she had made all the pastry and crusts that she could, reveling in having enough room to roll them out properly. Plus, the space was big enough that having the oven on at the hottest time of day didn't make her sweat like she was running a marathon. And Hunter's oven actually heated up to the proper temperatures and didn't have a weird hot spot in the back left corner like the oven in her apartment.

With her latest batch of oatmeal raisin cookies cooling on a rack, Brooke shook the final crumbs from the counter into the trash can and hung the rag back where she kept it. She grabbed a cookie, which split into two because it hadn't had the chance to fully cool, and scarfed it down as she walked into the attached living room.

"Ah, hot! Why do I always do that? You'd think I'd learn, but here we are," she said to Scratch, who didn't stir from his nap.

The little kitten was curled up in a furry ball in his bright green bed, taking advantage of a sunbeam coming through the window to sun himself. Scratch loved Hunter's house almost as much as Brooke did. There was much more room to sprint back and forth at two in the morning, as he loved to do, and so many more spots to sit and watch birds.

Brooke finished the last of her cookie as her phone buzzed in her shorts pocket. It was Travis, sending a message to everyone in their family group text.

Just handled a break-in on the north side. Be careful and lock your doors, the message read.

Brooke had to smile. Travis sent reminders like that from time to time, so she was used to the protective cop in him coming out in this way. He had always cared deeply about his family, so the texts weren't annoying to her at all. She figured she would worry and be a bit overprotective too if their roles were reversed.

She double-checked to make sure that Hunter's home security system was on, then grabbed her laptop and a stuffed catnip mouse for Scratch. The house had a patio that overlooked the water, and it had quickly become one of her favorite spots. She went out to the table, letting Scratch follow since he rarely left her side, and opened up her laptop.

The document she had open was blank aside from the words "bakery plan" written across the top. She gave Scratch the mouse toy, which he adored.

He chomped on it, rolling onto his back at her feet as she stared at the document.

"Must be nice to be a cat, huh?" she murmured to Scratch, who was already purring away like a miniature motorboat. "You don't have to worry about the ins and outs of starting a business. Or fears of messing up."

After the amazing shout out in Meredith's review of the inn, Brooke knew the time was right to start making serious plans for her bakery. Between the farmers' market, the guests at the inn, and her growing recipe book, she couldn't find an excuse *not* to go for it. She was a great baker. Plus, Angela and Lydia had opened their own business, and it was thriving. With some hard work, she could do the same.

She hadn't told anyone that she was serious about opening the bakery soon—she wanted to have something more concrete laid out before she did. But even if no one else knew about it yet, she had started thinking of the day she would open her own bakery as a "when" and not an "if."

Brooke swallowed and took a steadying breath, then started sketching out the plans that she had kept in her head for years.

CHAPTER TWENTY-TWO

When Jake had said he wanted to build a robot for one of his classes, Angela had told him that she was happy to help him out. But she hadn't thought much about what building a robot actually entailed. After all, Jake was only six years old—how hard could putting together a little boy's project be?

As it turned out, the project had been much more difficult than she'd expected.

She sighed and stared down at all the pieces of the robot on the floor in front of them. The instructions were made up of diagrams that didn't make any sense without a single word there to point her in the right direction. When she put together furniture or Lego figurines, she could at least make an educated guess. This was entirely new territory.

"Maybe it's supposed to go like this, Mommy," Jake said, putting a red piece against a blue piece. He cocked his head to the side and stared at it, just as lost as she was.

"I don't know, sweetheart." Angela ran a hand over his hair, trying to tamp down her frustration. "Why don't we take a little break so I can see if I can figure it out? I guess I'll look online."

"Okay!"

Jake wandered over to his toys, leaving Angela surrounded by the robot pieces. Her phone buzzed in her pocket, and just as she had hoped, it was Patrick, asking her how she was doing. She got off the floor, smiling to herself as she went to her laptop. She liked his check-in texts. He always seemed to know just when to send them to brighten her day.

I'm mostly fine, she sent back. *Struggling to put together a robot for Jake's summer school project. Do you happen to be good at reading indecipherable diagrams in instructions? I can put together furniture and sometimes Lego stuff, but this little robot is stumping me.*

Actually, yeah, he texted moments later. *I'm taking a break from writing and can come over to help if you want.*

Seriously? That would be amazing, thanks!

Angela sagged in relief after she hit send. Jake loved his new school. The school year had just started, and he was doing really well. She didn't want her inability to help him with this project make him less excited about his classes.

"Patrick is going to come by to help us with the robot," she told her son. "He's a lot better at this than I am."

"Patrick!" Jake's eyes lit up with happiness. "When will he be here?"

"Soon. Let me clean up a little before he comes over." Angela glanced around the room, which was in utter chaos—partially because of their attempts at putting together the robot, and partially because Jake's energetic nature meant he could create chaos almost anywhere.

Angela was used to cleaning up quickly though, so by the time Patrick arrived, everything looked more or less orderly. She'd smoothed her blonde hair into a neat ponytail but hadn't had time to change out of her yoga pants and t-shirt. But then again, she didn't really mind the idea of Patrick seeing her in a less "made up" state. The two of them had been getting very close, so she didn't feel like she needed to put on airs for him. He knew the *real* her—even the messy, complicated parts—and he seemed to like her just as she was.

"Hey! Thanks so much for coming." Angela gave him a hug after opening the door and ushering him inside. He smelled like the same soap that the inn had, and she briefly wondered if he'd gone out and purchased some for himself after he'd checked out.

"Of course. It's no problem." He squeezed her shoulder. "I'm my family's go-to guy for putting together toys at Christmas time, so hopefully this won't be too difficult."

"I hope so too. I think I'm more confused about this thing now than I was at the start." Angela laughed, then gestured toward the living room. "The robot's in here."

They walked into the living room of the innkeeper's residence, where Jake was fiddling with the pieces again. He waved frantically at Patrick, who said hello back.

"What do we have here?" Patrick asked, sitting down on the floor next to Jake. Angela sat down too, even though she knew she wouldn't be particularly helpful.

"A robot. Once he's built, he'll be really cool. If we turn the little knobby thing, he'll be able to walk by himself," Jake explained, pointing at the box.

"That's really cool." Patrick picked up the instructions, then looked at the box. "What kind of robot is he? Does he have a name?"

"His name is..." Jake bounced a few times on his knees, closing his eyes in concentration. "Bob? Bob the robot. He's very nice."

"Bob the robot, eh?" Patrick smiled. "Well, let's put him together so we can watch him walk around."

"Mommy's not good at putting him together," Jake said in a matter-of-fact way that made both Angela and Patrick laugh.

"No, I'm not." She picked up a little plastic gear and pushed it closer to the rest of the pile.

"But it's ok. My teacher says that it's okay to not be good at stuff sometimes." Jake picked up the box again and started playing with it, chewing absently on his lower lip. "That's why we go to school."

"Your teacher sounds like a smart person," Angela told him, tucking the tag into Jake's t-shirt and rubbing his back.

She loved his teacher. The class sizes in Jake's school on Marigold were much smaller than the ones in Philadelphia, so she felt like his teacher was able to give him much more attention than he ever could have gotten before.

"Yeah, she's really, really, *really* smart," Jake said.

"So let's impress her with Bob the robot." Patrick spread out the incomprehensible instructions. "We can work together. Let's get all the parts organized first."

Angela helped them organize the pieces into groups and double-checked whether the box had come with everything they needed. Then she sat back and let Patrick take over. As it turned out, he was much better at this kind of thing than she was. He and her son put together more pieces in five minutes than she and Jake had in thirty.

"Do you guys want something to drink?" Angela asked after a little while, standing up.

"Yes please!" Jake nodded, not taking his attention off Bob the robot's torso.

"Water would be great," Patrick added, putting down a piece that Angela had sworn was supposed to be part of the robot's head. "Thank you."

"Sure thing."

She went to the kitchen and filled a glass of water for Patrick and a plastic cup for Jake. Then she headed back to the living room, pausing in the doorway. The two of them were huddled together, Patrick murmuring instructions and Jake beaming whenever he put a piece together properly. Angela's heart warmed, the pleasant feeling spreading through her entire body. It was such a sweet sight.

She gave them their water and sat on the couch with her laptop as they finished. They were done before she could even get deep into her work.

"He's alive!" Jake said, cranking a little gear on the side of Bob the robot's hip. "Mommy, look at it!"

Angela closed her laptop and watched the robot shuffle across the carpet. Jake clapped with glee and went to go turn the robot's crank again.

"Great job, buddy!" Patrick grinned at him. "High five?"

Jake stopped turning the crank for a moment and gave Patrick a big high five. Patrick watched the robot shuffle back toward them with a satisfied smile.

Angela hadn't thought her affection for Patrick could grow anymore, but in that moment, she was almost overwhelmed by a wave of emotion. Even though Patrick didn't have any kids, he was clearly great with them. Jake was a sweet boy, but he rarely bonded with anyone like this outside of his own family.

"What do we say to Patrick for helping today?" Angela asked, hoping her melting heart wasn't too obvious.

"Thank you!" Jake gave Patrick another high five.

"No problem." Patrick stood up and stretched before joining Angela on the couch. He shook his head ruefully, gazing down at the little robot. "I forgot how complex some of these newer toys can be."

"You seemed to handle it easily. We probably would have been wrestling with it for another few hours." Angela glanced at her watch. "Though it's getting close to dinnertime—time flies. Do you want to stay? Lydia is out with Grant, so it'll just be the three of us."

Her heart fluttered a little at the thought. She and Patrick had never eaten dinner together, and it was one of her favorite ways to bond with people. Her turn to cook for her family dinners hadn't come up in a while, so she was happy to cook for someone besides Jake or Lydia.

Patrick's face lit up, his green eyes shining. "Sure, if it's not too much trouble."

"It's no problem at all, seriously. It'll be my way of saying thanks."

Angela went into the kitchen and started cooking while Patrick kept Jake occupied. The two of them put Bob away so that he would be ready to take to school and then sat at the kitchen table, working on coloring pages.

Jake had been crazy about pasta lately, which Angela didn't mind, so she started making spaghetti and meat sauce. It was easy to sneak extra vegetables into the sauce too, although Jake's palate had been expanding ever since their mood to Marigold. She hardly had to press him to chow down on a roasted carrot or a steamed green bean anymore.

Dinner was ready quickly, and they sat down to eat together at the table, with Angela sitting across from Patrick. Even though she knew her pasta recipe was good, she still watched him for his reaction when he took a bite of the dish she'd prepared.

"This is great. Thank you." He closed his eyes for a moment, as if trying to savor the flavors. "It's been a while since I've eaten amazing home-cooked food. I've never been a great cook, so I've been throwing together what I can in my new place."

She smiled. "I'm glad you like it. Are you all settled in at your house?"

"Yup, all settled. I love it. It's a really good fit for me," Patrick said. "And my new office is finally unpacked. It took me forever to get my last few books up on shelves, but I finally managed to do it. So now

I don't feel like I'm trapped in a sea of boxes as I work."

"So you've been able to work on your book? Have you done more outlining?" Angela asked, half because she was curious and half because she loved seeing Patrick's face light up when he talked about his creative projects.

"Yeah! It's going pretty well. I figured out my primary antagonist a little more, and the story shifted a bit. Now it's about a restauranteur who's caught up in some shady business."

Angela nodded, appreciating just how much he toned down the real plots of his books when he talked about them in front of Jake. "Shady business" probably meant all sorts of things that a six-year-old didn't need to know. She made a mental note to ask him more about it when Jake wasn't around.

"Is it like *Ratatouille*?" Jake asked, swinging his legs back and forth under the table. "There was a restaurant and a guy got in trouble in that movie."

Patrick and Angela exchanged a knowing smile, barely holding back laughter. Patrick's writing and *Ratatouille* were on completely different sides of the spectrum.

"A little bit, I guess," Patrick said.

"Mommy, can we watch *Ratatouille* again after

dinner?" Jake asked, his eyes going wide with excitement.

"All right." Angela wiped a little pasta sauce off his cheek. "Since you finished your homework, that sounds fine. You're welcome to stay, Patrick."

"Sure, I'd love to. I've never actually seen it before."

"How? *Everyone*'s seen *Ratatouille*," Jake said with a gasp. "Everyone in my whole class, and my teacher. And Grandma and Grandpa and Brooke and Travis."

"I don't know." Patrick chuckled. "I guess it's a good thing you brought it up, huh?"

"Yeah! It's my favorite."

Jake talked non-stop about what Patrick had been missing for the rest of dinner, giving away the entire plot—which, fortunately, Patrick didn't seem to mind. He kept up his stream of chatter all the way up until they settled down on the couch in the living room to finally watch the movie.

They pushed the coffee table aside so Jake could sit on the floor, since he always preferred to make a little fort out of blankets when they had movie nights. Angela and Patrick sat on the couch, and her heart gave a little thud in her chest as she settled in on the cushions.

The couch suddenly felt like a tiny loveseat to her. The softness of the cushions made Patrick's body dip toward hers, and it took a lot of willpower for her to not close the gap to cuddle up against him. She'd missed nights in like this, just watching movies and eating snacks with the people she cared about. She'd thought she had felt content in Marigold before, but having Patrick there made everything feel whole.

Angela had seen *Ratatouille* ten thousand times—or at least, that was what it felt like—and Jake had too, so watching it with someone who had never seen it before was a nice change of pace. By the time the movie was over, Jake had gone from fidgety to sleepy, lying on his side and barely keeping his eyes open.

"Let's get ready for bed, sweetheart," Angela murmured, hoisting Jake into her arms. She glanced over her shoulder to look at Patrick. "It won't take long."

"No worries, take your time," he said with an easy smile.

Angela helped Jake brush his teeth and put on his pajamas. The little boy was still so sleepy that his eyes were closed again almost as soon as his head hit the pillow. Angela tip-toed out of the room after making sure his night-light was turned on, though she doubted he would wake up until the morning.

She went back to the living room, her heart beginning to pound harder the moment she looked at Patrick again. His chestnut brown hair was a little disheveled, and something about the way the soft lighting in the living room hit him made Angela a little weak in the knees. He was still so handsome that she couldn't believe it.

The afternoon had been incredibly simple, but so *perfect* with him there. He blended right in and gave her home a warmth that she had never expected to feel so soon with anyone after ending her marriage to Scott. She hadn't been sure she'd ever feel it again at all.

Patrick stood when she walked back into the room, as if he was going to get ready to leave. But she couldn't let him go so soon.

They had agreed to take it slow. They had agreed to just be friends while they figured out what this thing was between them. But Angela didn't want to wait anymore. She didn't want to hold back.

The truth was, she *knew* what this thing between them was, and just because it had happened soon after her divorce didn't mean it wasn't real.

So she walked right up to Patrick and pulled him

into a gentle kiss before she could talk herself out of it.

* * *

Patrick stiffened for just an instant when Angela's lips met his. She had caught him by surprise, and for a moment, he couldn't believe this was really happening.

But his heart was beating too hard and fast for this to be a dream.

So he pulled the blonde-haired woman into his arms, sighing into the kiss.

Her lips were soft and sweet, and she felt so warm tucked against him. That warmth spread all through his body, radiating from his heart. He was finally holding her the way he'd wanted to for ages. It felt more than just right—it felt perfect. The whole afternoon had felt perfect, like he was exactly where he needed to be.

He broke the kiss after a beat, resting his forehead against hers for a moment before giving her another brief kiss.

"What happened to us just being friends?" he asked, chuckling and playing with her ponytail. He never wanted to let her go.

"I think we waited long enough, don't you?" She looked up at him, her hands still resting on his chest. "I know how I feel about you, and I hope you feel the same about me. Just because it's soon doesn't mean it's not right."

"That's true." Patrick kissed her forehead and pulled her closer, inhaling the addictive vanilla scent of her shampoo. "I don't know how I was able to hold out this long. Every single text you sent me made my day, and I couldn't get enough. I could hardly focus."

"Really?" She beamed. "I felt the same way. Every time my phone beeped, I'd grab it right away and hope it was a message from you. Brooke totally caught on to my crush when she saw me reading one of your texts."

Patrick laughed, running his fingers through the soft hair at the nape of her neck. "I probably looked the same way, but no one was around to witness it."

They went quiet for a few moments, holding each other and savoring the feeling of being in each other's arms at last. Angela rested her ear against his chest, where he was sure she could hear his heart still pounding at a fast clip.

"I'm a little nervous about doing this," he admitted after a while. "I haven't been with anyone but Aubrey since high school, and I don't want to mess it up."

"I'm nervous too, don't worry. And you won't mess it up." She cupped his face, running her thumbs along his cheeks as he gazed down at her "We both want this, and we both really care about each other. If we run into a problem, we can work through it."

Patrick reached up to take one of her hands, clasping it in his in the small space between their bodies. "I like the idea that we're both jumping into the unknown together. It makes the leap a lot less scary."

Angela's smile got even wider, and he had to kiss her again.

He had a feeling this was the beginning of something truly wonderful.

CHAPTER TWENTY-THREE

Angela took a deep breath of the fresh sea air and smiled as she walked down the beach. She had been smiling almost non-stop in the week since she and Patrick had first kissed. They had gone out on a casual ice cream date and a walk since then, but that was it so far.

Still, it had been the best date Angela had ever been on. They'd talked about anything and everything with ease, laughing and joking around as if they'd been close for years. All the expensive restaurants and plays she had been to on dates in the past couldn't compare to a nice conversation and some red velvet ice cream with the man who was quickly becoming one of her favorite people in the world.

She waved to Brooke as her younger sister came out of Hunter Reed's house in a sweatshirt and leggings. It was early October, and Summer was over, but it was still just warm enough to be nice out.

"Morning!" Angela called.

"Good morning!" Brooke hugged her. Then she pulled back and eyed Angela up and down. "You look like you're in a good mood. Being in a new relationship suits you well."

Angela flushed. "It really does. It's so nice. I forgot how good it feels to be with someone who really gets you."

"I'm so happy for you, Angie." Brooke squeezed her shoulder and then turned and started to walk down the beach. Angela fell into step beside her. "Have you guys been going out a lot?"

"We went out for ice cream, but that's it. We want to take it pretty slow still since both of our divorces have just been finalized." Angela shrugged. "We aren't in a hurry anyway. It just feels so good to have that weight off my chest. I was going crazy trying to hold my feelings back. I felt like I had a huge sign on my back that screamed that I liked him."

"I bet." Brooke laughed. "If you looked even half

as thrilled to talk to him in person as you did when he texted, everyone would have caught on in an instant."

"Will you ever let me live that down?" Angela shook her head, chuckling.

"Eventually, but not today." Brooke bumped her shoulder against Angela's. "What else would you expect from your younger sister?"

"True, true." Angela rolled her eyes a little, nodding. "Anyway, it really is better to have all of our feelings out there. Now we can actually explore where things are going between us."

"What does Scott think?" Brooke asked after a pause.

Angela let out a slow breath. She had spoken with Scott over a video call with Jake a couple days ago, but it hadn't felt like the right time to tell him. He and Jake had been having a great time talking, and she hadn't wanted to veer them off course to talk about her life. And she wanted to ease Jake into the idea that she and Patrick were dating, even though she knew Jake adored Patrick already.

"I haven't told him yet," Angela said, tucking her hands into the pockets of her sweatshirt. "I mean, I will soon. I want him to know what's going on with me, especially since we're still connected through Jake, but it feels so strange."

"Don't let the weirdness stop you. It'll be good for Scott to see that you're moving on, and that it's with a man Jake really likes."

"Yeah, that's also true. There's a lot going on that we have to take care of first. Scott really wants Jake to come visit him in Philly, which I want too. Even though he wasn't a great husband, he's a good father."

"Yeah. I have to give him that too. *Grudgingly*." Brooke sighed.

"I definitely don't want him to feel like I'm trying to push Patrick on Jake either. And I don't want Jake to feel like Patrick is trying to replace his dad."

Angela ran a hand through her hair, looking down the beach at a flock of seagulls as she spoke. A bit of lingering anxiety sat in her chest, but it went away when she thought about what Patrick was really like. He wouldn't do something like that.

"I don't know Patrick that well, but he doesn't seem like that kind of guy," Brooke pointed out, as if she had read Angela's mind.

"No, he isn't. Jake really likes him too. They get along amazingly well, so I think things will work out." Angela let her shoulders relax a bit. It really would be okay.

"I hope so," Brooke said. "You deserve a nice guy in your life."

The two walked in peaceful silence for a while. With the summer season over, many of the tourists had cleared out, leaving the beach mostly empty besides other people taking their morning walks, and clusters of seagulls huddled against the breeze. Angela couldn't believe they were heading into the peak of the fall. So much had changed for her in the past few months.

"How is house-sitting at Hunter's place going?" she asked.

"Ah, it's so nice. And really easy." Brooke made a contented sound in her throat. "It's so calm and quiet. I've never slept so well in my life. The guest room bed is like a perfect little cocoon. Since it's gotten cooler, I've been taking more baths, and with a bath bomb and some candles, it feels like I've been transported to a spa."

"That sounds so amazing. I'd kill for a spa day."

"Oh! We should have one with Mom and Lydia." Brooke perked up at the idea. "I heard good things about that new place near the Sweet Creamery—they do massages, mani/pedis and facials."

"What a perfect location. Finishing up a spa day and going right to get ice cream sounds like my dream day."

"I know, right? Let me write this down so I won't forget, and we won't let it slide by because we're busy." Brooke pulled out her phone and made a note. "Also, all the relaxing I've done at Hunter's place has given me a lot of space to think—so more chilling out wouldn't hurt."

"Yeah?" Angela looked over at Brooke, who had trapped her bottom lip between her teeth as if she were nervous.

"Yeah. I've been working on my plans for a bakery more seriously. I mean, Hunter's massive kitchen gives me a ton of space to work on recipes, but I've also been looking into small business loans and things like that." Brooke smiled, although she still seemed a little anxious. "It's a lot, but I really want to go for it. Right now, I'm envisioning it as a small place, but who knows what I'll come up with after I see what's possible?"

"Wow. I'm so thrilled for you!" Angela squeezed Brooke's arm.

"You are?"

"Of course I am. It's your dream, and I want you

to succeed," Angela assured her sister. "I'll help in any way I can, okay?"

Brooke's smile lost its anxious edge. She glanced out at the water, then back at Angela. "Sounds like a plan."

CHAPTER TWENTY-FOUR

Lydia sat back in her office chair as she hit "send" on an email to the editor of a local travel magazine who wanted to send one of his writers to visit the inn. It was one of several media requests they'd gotten over the past several days, to everyone's delight. Meredith Walters' review had spread even farther than they'd dreamed it might. Bookings were up, and more positive reviews from guests were rolling in.

Since Holly had gone back to school after her quick visit with Nicolas, Lydia had been able to throw herself into work at the inn again.

Finally, she felt like she had some steady footing.

Their day-to-day schedule didn't feel so much like climbing a massive hill anymore, and she was able to take more time to breathe. Having more time to dedicate to the administrative side of things was the best thing that could have happened for their business.

After sending a couple more quick emails, Lydia checked their online bookings to schedule the front desk shifts for the upcoming weeks. She scrolled through... and kept scrolling, her eyes widening. She clicked back and looked again, just to be sure that she was seeing things correctly. In mid-October, there was a weekend on the calendar where every room would be fully booked. It was the first time that had happened—the first time they would have no vacancies.

Lydia pushed back from the desk and grabbed her phone, texting Angela and Kathy to come back into the office.

"Hey, guess what?" she asked excitedly when they entered a moment later.

"What? Is it a good thing?" Angela asked, looking mildly panicked. Kathy looked a little alarmed too.

"A really good thing." Lydia waved them over and pointed to the computer. "We're booked solid for an upcoming weekend!"

Angela's and Kathy's expressions of worry dissolved, replaced by massive smiles. They hugged each other, then hugged Lydia too when she stood up. Lydia couldn't stop smiling. Months ago, when they'd felt like they were drowning in all the work associated with opening a new business and getting it off the ground, she and Angela had wished for a fully booked weekend. They'd hoped desperately for one.

Back then, the idea had felt abstract and almost impossible. But now, it was real.

"I can't believe we did it!" Angela blinked, running her hand through her brown hair as she stared at the computer screen. "I'm looking right at it, and it still feels surreal."

"I know, right?" Lydia looked at the bookings too. Then she glanced up at their employee. "We can't thank you enough for all your help. If you hadn't been here, I don't know if we would have had the time to do what we had to do to get ahead."

"Oh, stop." The redhead smiled, waving her hand as if she were brushing off the compliment. "You guys did most of the work. I just did what I could."

"Well, you did a lot." Angela squeezed Kathy's arm.

"I think this moment deserves some celebration muffins, don't you think?" Kathy asked, grinning.

"It absolutely does." Lydia laughed.

Kathy had become one of Brooke's biggest fans and took every available opportunity for a celebratory treat. It was Friday? Time to celebrate with scones. A customer told them that they hadn't had a better time in years? They had to enjoy the good news with a cupcake or two to congratulate themselves.

Lydia didn't mind in the slightest. It was nice to have some more positive energy in the inn, and Kathy was already going above and beyond in her role.

"I'll go grab them!" The quirky, energetic woman was out the door in an instant. "Be right back!"

A short while later, Kathy came back with some morning glory muffins and napkins. The three women toasted with the muffins, laughing happily before taking their first bites.

They polished off the muffins just as Grant appeared in the doorway. He was wearing a flannel shirt over a *Hamlin Landscaping* t-shirt, jeans, and clean boots, like he was on his way to a landscaping job. Lydia felt the zing of happiness that always went through her when she looked at Grant. It didn't matter if he was all dressed up or if he was covered in dirt—he was attractive no matter what.

"What's going on in here?" he asked. He often

popped into the back office when he knew Lydia was working and kept her company, so no one was surprised to see him.

Lydia stood up and rushed over to him, throwing her arms around his shoulders and kissing him. He managed to stay upright and kissed her back, chuckling against her lips.

"Sorry for almost taking you down like a linebacker. We just learned that the inn is fully booked for an entire weekend this fall. It's the first time that's happened!" Lydia clutched his upper arms so she wouldn't jump up and down like a kid.

"That's amazing." His eyes danced as he pulled her into a hug and squeezed. "Congrats to all of you."

"Thank you!" Angela beamed.

"Sorry we don't have any celebratory muffins left for you," Kathy said, cleaning crumbs from her fingers. "I grabbed the last three morning glory ones for us."

"No worries. I've been spoiled with Brooke's muffins this whole week anyway."

Lydia had given him a bunch to take home after Brooke had made an extra batch. They were his favorites, and Lydia loved the way his face lit up when she did little things like that for him. She didn't mind the kiss he usually gave her as a thank you either.

"Mind if I steal Lydia for a walk?" Grant asked, sliding an arm around her waist.

"Yeah, go ahead. We've got things under control here." Angela shooed them off. "Go have fun."

"Let me get a sweater—it's getting chilly." Lydia stood from behind the desk and held up a finger to her new beau before slipping out of the room. She went to the front desk to find her sweater just as the phone rang.

"Hello, this is the Beachside Inn. My name is Lydia. How may I help you?" she asked, propping the phone between her ear and her shoulder as she shrugged on her cardigan.

"Oh, perfect! I'm glad I caught you. This is Meredith Walters."

"Meredith! Hi!" Lydia leaned against the desk, surprised. "I'm so glad you called. Thank you so much for your lovely review. Our business has really picked up since it was published."

"I'm glad to hear it! Thank you for a lovely stay." There was a smile in Meredith's voice that Lydia could hear even over the phone. "I loved hearing about how the inn was a fresh start for you and Angela. It really resonated with me. I got divorced a few years ago and found a fresh start of my own not long ago. I met a wonderful man, and we've gotten engaged."

"Congratulations! That's so exciting," Lydia said.

"Thank you! That's why I was calling, actually. I loved Marigold Island so much that I'd like to have our wedding there. It's such a beautiful place, and everyone I met there made me feel so at home. It would be a small, intimate event since we've both been married before, and we'd love to book the entire inn for it next summer."

Lydia's mouth fell open, and she nearly dropped the phone. She wasn't sure if she was mishearing or not. "The whole inn? All the rooms?"

"Yes, if that's possible."

"It definitely is! We would be delighted to host you and your guests." Lydia sat down at the front desk, her heart racing a thousand miles an hour and a grin spreading across her face. "Do you have a date in mind?"

Meredith told her the rough time of year they were planning on, and they found a date that was clear of bookings. As Lydia put Meredith's information into the computer, Grant stepped into the lobby, looking at her with a question in his eyes.

Lydia held up her hand to tell him to give her a second.

She finished the booking and thanked Meredith again before hanging up.

"You won't believe what just happened," she told him, a wave of giddy happiness washing through her. "I thought things were looking up for the inn before, but this just took it to a whole new level. I think we're really on our way."

* * *

Grant laced his fingers in Lydia's as they walked out the front door of the inn and down the beach. She was practically buzzing with excitement, looking truly overjoyed. He loved seeing her this happy, doing what she was passionate about. Nothing made her look more beautiful.

"The anticipation is killing me, Lyds," he said with a gentle laugh. "Or will I have to wait until the end of the walk to find out what exactly happened on that call?"

"Sorry, I'm just trying to wrap my head around it all." Lydia laughed softly. "That was Meredith Walters on the phone. She just booked the whole inn for her wedding in the summer!"

"That's incredible." Grant squeezed her hand, pride bubbling up in his chest.

"It is! I can't believe we didn't think of weddings before. It could be a whole new way to grow the business." Lydia seemed to have an extra lightness in her step, and her joy was contagious. "People love having beach weddings around here."

"It's a beautiful space. They could have the ceremonies in the back area or even out on the beach in front of the inn." Grant looked out at the sand in front of them, imagining couples tying the knot and heading back to the Beachside Inn to celebrate. It was easy to picture.

"Yeah," she agreed, looking up at him. "I can't believe someone of her caliber wants to have her wedding here. At our little inn."

"I can. You and Angela have made it something incredibly special."

"Thank you. That means a lot."

As she spoke, Lydia's smile turned a little shy. She bit her lip and glanced out at the water, and Grant rubbed his thumb over the back of her hand. He wanted her to know he was proud of her and in awe of what she'd done, even if she had a hard time taking compliments with ease.

"It's funny. Meredith told me that she was

getting a fresh start too, which was why the story of how we opened the inn resonated with her so much," Lydia said. "It's almost the theme of the inn at this point. People can come to the Beachside to start things anew or find peace and happiness when they're recovering from heartbreak. It's all about starting over. Maybe it can make a new chapter in life feel less scary for people."

Grant nodded, studying her profile as she looked off into the distance, a little starry-eyed. Seeing her look so hopeful and excited always stirred something in his chest, something that made everything in his world feel just right. He had felt it for a while, but as he listened to Lydia talk, he knew he could finally put words to the feeling out loud.

He stopped and pulled her into his arms. She stiffened a little in surprise, then relaxed into his embrace, wrapping her arms around him and resting her head on his chest. Eventually, she lifted her head, still looking slightly confused as to what had prompted their sudden stop. Grant took the opportunity to plant a soft kiss on her lips.

"I love you, Lydia," he said quietly, tucking her hair behind her ear.

Her beautiful green eyes widened, then glistened with tears. "You do?"

"I do. I have for a while, I think. It's been growing inside my chest day by day, but listening to you talk about all of this made me realize just how much I adore you."

Lydia beamed, blinking back tears. "I love you too."

He cupped her face and pressed his lips to hers, giving the kiss everything he had. It had been so long since Grant had felt this mixture of pure joy and love. He had missed it, and being able to share the feeling with Lydia was better than anything he could have dreamed about even six months ago.

Lydia was right about the inn. If it hadn't been for that open house, he probably wouldn't have met her. And he probably would have continued going through the motions of living and not getting anywhere, lost in lingering grief. His life would have passed him by.

Lydia had given him a second chance at life, one that he'd never even known he needed. He could tell her that he loved her every day—and he certainly planned to—but he had no idea how to put the magnitude of his gratitude that they'd met into words. Maybe one day he'd find out how.

After a few moments of contented silence, they

laced their fingers together again and continued their walk.

For a long time after Annie's death, Grant's future had seemed muddled and cloudy. He hadn't been able to look past the present moment, focused only on getting by day to day.

But he felt like he could see his future clearly now, and it was filled with happiness and love.

ABOUT THE AUTHOR

Fiona writes sweet, feel-good contemporary women's fiction and family sagas with a bit of romance.

She hopes her characters will start to feel like old friends as you follow them on their journeys of love, family, friendship, and new beginnings. Her heartwarming storylines and charming small-town beach settings are a particular favorite of readers.

When she's not writing, she loves eating good meals with friends, trying out new recipes, and finding the perfect glass of wine to pair them with. She lives on the East Coast with her husband and their two trouble-making dogs.

Follow her on her website, Facebook, or Bookbub.

Sign up to receive her newsletter, where you'll get free books, exclusive bonus content, and info on her new releases and sales!

ALSO BY FIONA BAKER

The Marigold Island Series

The Beachside Inn

Beachside Beginnings

Beachside Promises

Beachside Secrets

Beachside Memories

Beachside Weddings

Made in the USA
Las Vegas, NV
27 November 2023